The Castle On Herbert Way

Heart-pounding adventures of three precocious young girls, who are first cousins and best friends forever. ♥

Marie Bennett

authorHOUSE®

AuthorHouse™
1663 Liberty Drive
Bloomington, IN 47403
www.authorhouse.com
Phone: 1-800-839-8640

Published by AuthorHouse   01/30/2015

ISBN: 978-1-4772-9793-3 (sc)
ISBN: 978-1-4772-9794-0 (e)

Print information available on the last page

Library of Congress Control Number: 2012923281

Any people depicted in stock imagery provided by Thinkstock are models, and such images are being used for illustrative purposes only. Certain stock imagery © Thinkstock.

This book is printed on acid-free paper.

This book is dedicated to Rosemary my mother, and DeeDee my daughter who are the most precious gifts of my life. I am also grateful for an awesome family without whom I would have no inspiration.

Table of Contents

Prologue

Diary,

First of all, I want to begin by saying that a diary is not an appropriate birthday present. It's not everyday that a young girl turns a mature twelve, you know. I don't even like writing, so what would I do with a dumb old diary? No offense, Diary, but what I really wanted was that blueberry lip gloss and nail polish set. It's on sale right now at the Dollar Discount Store in town. For weeks I've been telling Queen Fannie exactly how much that blueberry set cost. I even told her what aisle it was on. Plus they gave you a one week supply of that sweet blueberry gum at no extra cost. Now, you can't beat that, you get more bang for your buck. That's why I was so excited before I opened my present because I knew exactly what I thought it would be. You know something that I would actually use. Instead, I opened up this beautifully wrapped gift and found you, Diary. Again, no offense, but this has made me nervous, this is an important day. I had high expectations. It would have been a perfect day. I could be painting my finger nails and my toe nails right now with my fabulous blueberry nail gloss. And oh the flavor of that blueberry gum would have been a heavenly sweet treat in my mouth right now. And so with much regret, my idea of fun does not involve writing in a diary. Have I made myself clear? I HATE YOU, DUMB OLD DIARY!

Wow, I feel a lot better now that I've told you my honest to goodness real feelings. But I can't tell Queen Fannie 'because she thinks it's "mahvahlous" to write your ideas and thoughts in a diary. That's the way she talks. Everything is just "mahvahlous". She should know better than to give a young lady a diary, with her weird self. Although, I must admit that the leopard cover is cool. It kind'f reminds me of her, 'cause animal print is her favorite print. I do like that she has my name engraved in gold with sprinkles of gold glitter on the front, and the pages are oh, so, so wonderful, they're in my favorite color—baby blue! Now it's not because my last name is Blue, but because me and my cousins just like that color. It's a dreamy color, you know.

Oh and before I forget, my whole name is Silky Blue. I'm a sixth grader at Sloan County Elementary School. English is not my favorite subject, but I am a good student. I have two girl cousins and one boy cousin. I'm the oldest and the tallest of my girl cousins. Their names are Brianna and Tiffany. The three of us were all born in the same year. Stuck-on-himself Jabari is the only boy, but I'll tell you about the girl's first 'cause they're more fun. Do you wan'na know something really interesting? Well . . . even though me and Tiffany and Brianna are blood cousins, we don't look the same at all. We don't even look like we're related, but we are very close. To show our solidarity, we dress like three peas in pod almost every day. If we didn't, how would everyone know that we are cousins and best friends too?

Diary, I'll tell you about Tiffany because she is the next oldest. Tiffany's birthday is two months from now. Then, she will be twelve just like me, but that is where our similarities end. Because Tiffany's mother, Aunt Ruth, is of Irish decent, Tiffany's skin is pale, and her hair is straight, brown, and ends about to her shoulders. She has to wear braces and is on the pudgy side. She calls herself big boned. No matter what she calls it, she's bigger than me and Brianna. And she is the only one who knows what she wants to be when she grows up. Tiffany wants to be a singing diva and live in New York. Tiffany does have a gorgeous voice. When we sing in the church choir at Greater Light Baptist, her voice really stands out.

Last year, Queen Fannie bought her a light blue karaoke recorder with a cool CD player and a microphone attached. She records her voice when she sings. Also, she practices at home by sitting on the washing machine when it's on the spin cycle. It sounds dumb, but now she has a pretty voice with plenty of vibrato. Tiffany taught me that word vibrato. Because she is a diva-in-training, she really knows her music. She knows what she likes and what she doesn't like. She doesn't just sing any old song. Rhythm and blues and Gospel are her favorite kinds of music or should I say, genre. Lucky for her, Queen Fannie has a large collection of R&B and Gospel music, so we always listen to Queen Fannie's music, especially her old Diana Ross CDs. "Baby Love" is Queen Fannie's favorite song, and it's ours, too. Enough about Tiffany let me tell you about my other best friend and girl cousin.

Her name is Brianna and her birthday is three weeks after Tiffany's. Brianna's dad, Uncle Ned is Mexican and is married to my Aunt Mable. But for now, Uncle Ned and Aunt Mable are estranged. At least, that's what my Momma said. She said it means that they are separated for now, but they're still husband and wife, and they still love each other. My Momma would know because Aunt Mable is her sister and they talk on the phone almost every day.

Brianna's most prized possession is a pretty bracelet made of turquoise stones that Uncle Ned gave her. It came from Mexico where he grew up. She wears it only on special occasions. Brianna doesn't know what she wants to be when she grows up, but I can tell you, Diary, she's a real neat freak who loves to read. That's why Queen Fannie always buy her books for her birthday. She's extra neat now 'cause she thinks her parents are estranged 'cause she didn't make her bed up just right; it was always on the lumpy side. She's such a silly goose.

The aunts and uncles in our family say she's the most me-tho-di-cal of the three of us. And lately, she's been the most emotional, but Brianna loves being with me and Tiffany. She might think twice when she's reading a good book, but we always win because we always have fun when we're together.

Brianna is brown skinned and looks a lot like her father, but her hair is not as straight as Uncle Ned's; hers is long and frizzy with lots of waves. She wears it in one thick braid that hangs all the way down to the middle of her back.

She's the youngest and the smallest of us and the only one who has an older brother. I call him Stuck-on-himself Jabari. I call him that 'cause he gets on my nerves, thinkin' he's cute and all and, we like to spy on him when he's looking at himself in the mirror, smiling and turning from one side to the other, and dabbin' Vaseline on those fine hairs under his nose. Diary, he's so full of himself. He can stare at his profile for hours. I get nauseated just thinking about it. He loves to talk about all the girls who's sweatin' him. He's such a moron. I'm glad he's away at college.

See, I have to keep reminding him that he has a Mr. Peanut Head just so he won't think he's all that cute. Now, I'm gonna tell you a secret, Diary. If he wasn't my cousin, I'd be sweatin' him, too, 'cause he sure is fine . . . for real! Now, to be honest, my whole family is very good-looking. And it all started with my grandparents. Now as for me, I look like my parents, Leon and Freda and both of my parents are African American, so I'm good looking too, strong legs, thick hair and all!

Dear and Grandpa were the heads of the Busby family. They were married for a long time and had four kids. My Momma and her siblings called their mother Dear. And that's what me and my cousins called her, too. Both of my grandparents are buried in the cemetery behind the Greater Light Baptist Church, Reverend Katrill is the senior pastor there. My Momma wears a picture of my grandparents in an old locket around her neck everyday.

Queen Fannie is the oldest. My Momma is next to the oldest. Aunt Mable, who is Brianna's mom, was born third, and then came Uncle Jimmy, the youngest. He was Tiffany's dad. Aunt Ruth and Uncle Jimmy were married, but he died a year after Tiffany was born. Everybody says Tiffany is the spittin' image of Dear and Uncle Jimmy, only she has a white complexion.

It's strange that Tiffany never misses her dad. I think it's because she doesn't remember him. Me and Brianna don't remember him, either. If my daddy wasn't around, I'd miss him 'cause I'm used to having him around, even though he burps loud and all . . . oh it's gross sometime. Tiffany thinks my daddy is cool and wants a daddy of her own, she doesn't care if he does burps.

Dear and Grandpa Busby raised their four kids in a big new house, it's the house that Grandpa built. The street was named Herbert Way after our grandpa Herbert. He built the house by himself when He and Dear were newly weds. It was so big and so pretty people around town called grandpa a master architect, even though he was really only a mail man, by trade.

Me and my cousin's call it the castle because it's the largest house on the block with the most land. We spend a lot of crazy fun there. The castle is not the gothic type you see in the movies; it's just a plain old big house, with a lot of drafty windows and a creaky staircase. So Diary when I mention the castle, you'll know what I'm talking about, I'll only call it the castle when I'm writing in you, that is, if I decide to continue to share my juicy secrets in you. It's such a waste of time writing in a diary.

Well anyway, the castle is where our family gathers for important occasions. It has loads of old family treasures and heirlooms throughout the house. It tells us a lot about who we are and where we came from. Pictures of our family members and ancestors are displayed all around and some old pictures are stuffed in different shoe boxes around the coffee table. The wedding albums of all the family members are stacked high on the end table in the living room. At the bottom of the stack are Dear and Grandpa's album. Soon, Queen Fannie and Uncle Schine's will be there, too, right on the top.

Our castle and everything surrounding it is like a mini museum of our family history because it was made with love. One of my favorite things about the castle is the gazebo in the backyard. Grandpa built it for Dear after he completed the house. They used to spend the warm evenings sitting in the gazebo while babysitting me. I'd take catnaps in my white bassinet while Dear cro-chet-ed and Grandpa smoked his expensive cigars. I know this 'cause my Momma told me so. See, my Momma always tells me everything. Now, the gazebo is where me and my cousins hold all our secret meetings. We call it our headquarters.

A tall pecan tree near the gazebo keeps the noisy squirrel family well fed. They run up and down the tree at least ten times a day. There's also a big vegetable garden in the back. It's the largest vegetable garden me and my cousins have ever seen. Every kind of vegetable you can name grows back there. Plus, there's a blueberry patch (our favorite fruit) right between the squash and black-eyed peas and rows and rows of neatly planted collard greens. Oh, Queen Fannie calls them her bouquets of collards, she loves her collard greens! I think there are more vegetables back there than Mr. Spiegel's Deli and Supermarket has in his produce section, but the Deli has the best candy section ever. He has the kind that you dream about while you're sitting in a boring class.

Now, Queen Fannie lives in the castle by herself. She doesn't have any children, so she calls my cousins and me her angels. Neva Schine is the man she's going to marry. We call him Uncle Schine because he's known us from the day we were born. Uncle Schine is of mixed heritage, too. His last name is pronounced shine . . . like the sunshine! I guess the only thing that bothers me is that Queen Fannie is a whole head taller than he is and they're old already! Brides and grooms are supposed to be young in age and young at heart! Oh well, that's the way we think it should be, but we're happy for them anyway.

Oh . . . I didn't tell you, but we secretly refer to our Aunt Fannie as Queen Fannie because she lives in the castle, and you know every castle must have a queen! So I'll refer to our Aunt Fannie as Queen Fannie when I'm writing in you, okay—but only if I'm not angry with her. Okay?

Now the queen truly is a nice person. She doesn't have a car, she rides her bike everywhere and has an antique shop which we sometimes call a junk shop 'cause it's truly junky. She has one employee. That's Ms. Hazel, her long time friend. We call her Ms. Hazel Nut 'cause she is a nut. She's probably the only woman in the whole wide world who wears two inch heels, with white sports socks while jogging. And that's not all, she's a strange lady, I know for a fact that she's strange, you've probably never met anyone like her before, she's a mess . . . more about her later.

I want to tell you one more thing about Queen Fannie. It's not about the flashy blonde wigs she wears or about her two dumb cats, Pearl and Earl. It's about how she talks about the spirits of my grandparents who she says still lives in the castle. They lived in the castle all their married lives, and Queen Fannie says they never left. She talks to them anytime she wants, especially when she has a problem too difficult to solve. Now, that's really spooky.

Dang! I almost forgot to tell you about the most magical room in the castle. It's up in the Queen's attic. I won't forget to tell you about the miracles that take place there for me and my cousins. See . . . I told you it was a castle. It's the only castle on Herbert Way.

Wait a minute . . . wait a minute, wait a hot minute! I can't believe I'm writing my business in a dumb old diary. I like telling my secrets to my cousins, and they like telling me theirs at the headquarters you know, but something tells me these smooth baby blue pages are hungry for more of my juicy secrets and probably my beautiful poetry too. Yes, I'm a poet, I didn't tell you that. But I am. I might create one for you Diary, but only if I feel like it. And oh, I won't forget to tell you about Cool Aid either; he's my heart throb. Ooops, I mean umm . . . he's my special friend only 'cause my momma said I'm too young to have a boyfriend.

So . . . okay now, this is enough Dairy, I'll probably forget about you tomorrow and the next day after that, 'cause you're dumb and boring but if I feel like sharing, I'll look for your leopard printed cover with my name engraved in gold.

Silky

Chapter One

Silky

Diary,

I'm writing from our den, sitting in my daddy's big brown leather recliner. When I push it all the way back, my feet don't go over the edge like my daddy's do. This is where my daddy makes all his major decisions, reads the sports pages, or just stares at the humongous flat screen TV he bought my momma for their anniversary.

As usual, my momma is in the kitchen. That's where she goes through her favorite magazines sitting at the kitchen table. She likes to look at pictures of kitchen makeovers while fanning her face. She uses the fan she got from the back of a pew from the church 'cause she gets hot flashes much more now than ever. She says she's going through "the change". My momma is forty-seven years old and very pretty. She dyes her hair chestnut brown to cover the gray. My daddy has a shiny forehead and a receding hairline. His forehead seems to get larger and shinier as he gets older.

Queen Fannie is planning to have a big wedding. Me and my cousins are going to be the bridesmaids, and we want to dress like the bridesmaids in the bridal magazines.

Now I've been thinking a lot about writing in this diary. I really don't think it's gonna work out. I mean, you know, this is okay and all, but I just don't treasure a diary like I would have treasured matching nail polish and the lip gloss set.

Did I tell you that I'm in class 6-1 at Sloan County Elementary School? I'm in the same classroom as Camisha Tolbertson. She's not real bad; she's just a nuisance who speaks her mind. Sometimes, she does go overboard and say funny or rude things, I laugh at them and sometimes I don't. But her mouth and behavior gets her in trouble big time.

My homeroom teacher is Ms. Thunder. She's a Native American from the Sioux tribe. She's nice, but she has a backside that's bigger than any teacher in the ENTIRE WORLD. I'm talkin' humongous. You know what? I bet you can put my Momma's backside together with all my aunts' backsides, and theirs still wouldn't be as big as Ms. Thunder's. Diary, it's seriously big.

Tiffany and Brianna are in Mr. Nicolson's class together and that class is on the other side of the hall near the library.

I got 'a go now. I'll try to write some more tomorrow, if I feel like wasting some more time, okay?

"It'll be one o'clock before you know it. I want to make sure we're on time for your fitting. Baby girl, be ready to go to your Aunt Fannie's house when I'm done, okay?" Freda didn't wait for an answer. Instead, she continued talking, "I'm going to touch up the gray around the edges and the kitchen area and treat myself to a quick shampoo. The fitting is for one o'clock. Don't forget."

As Silky heard the water rushing through the pipes, she continued to write really fast. She wanted to finish her thoughts for the morning in a most thorough way. After she completed her thoughts, she massaged her tired writing fingers where the blue ink pen made red marks. She gently closed the diary, placing it on top of the picture of Cool Aid holding the trophy he had received for winning the oratorical contest at school for the second year in a row.

Soon, she heard the old hair dryer blowing out hot air. It was unusually loud. Silky knew it was only a matter of time before her mother would be ready to go. Freda was always punctual. Even though Silky had never answered her mother's last question, she asked her own question loud enough for her mother to hear over the hair dryer, "Momma, where's Daddy? Is he coming, too?"

"No, I don't think so, dear. He'll probably stay home and watch the game. We'll take the two seater today."

The noisy hair dryer stopped as Silky stared at herself in the mirror. She wondered if the red spot on her chin was going to turn into a pimple. Freda was still talking loudly.

"I believe Mrs. Goldberg, you know the rich Jewish woman from Hillywood? She sold an eighteenth century wedding dress to Fannie to sell at her antique shop. It's supposed to be a rare find, imbedded with jewels and all. Why, I understand the dress weighs five pounds or more. No telling where Mrs. Goldberg got it from. Fannie loved it so much that she decided to have Mrs. Crump tailor it for her. She chose it to be her wedding dress as her something old. You know the old saying, 'Something old, something new, something borrowed, and something blue', right?"

"No. I have never heard of that before," Silky said, not interested and half-listening.

"On the day of your wedding, the bride is supposed to have all four of those items in her possession, but you know your Aunt Fannie. She has such strange taste. I just hope it's a presentable dress because I don't want her to make a spectacle out of herself, embarrassing the family and all. Sweetie, do you have any idea what time the wedding is supposed to start?"

"No," Silky said again.

"Well, I hope it starts with the hands on the clock going up. That brings the newlyweds good luck, you know? Anyway, Fannie mentioned that Mrs. Crump is very time conscientious, and she's supposed to be the best seamstress in Sloan County. Have you met her yet, dear?"

"No, Ma, but I'm ready to go," Silky answered. She couldn't wait to visit the Castle. It was always like a mini family reunion with lots of food. Of course, all of the aunts would be there. They always were. This time, they would gather for the business of picking out bridesmaid dresses. For the three girls, it was always the business of fun. Silky couldn't wait to see her cousins.

Chapter Two

Something Old

Diary,

My parents named me Silky 'cause my skin was smooth as silk and a pretty chocolate brown when I was born. Busby is my Momma's maiden name. Blue is my daddy's sir name, so we are the Blue family—Leon, Freda, and Silky. Daddy's sir name keeps us glued together as a family.

Little Silky Blue is what my daddy calls me when he's real proud of me, like the time I made the honor roll in school. He grinned and said, "That's my Little Silky Blue. She's smart just like her daddy."

You know, I don't want to hurt my daddy's feelings, but I really think my Momma is a little smarter than he is . . . well, maybe a lot smarter. I don't remember him ever winning an argument with her.

I have another confession to make, Diary. Sometimes, I'm embarrassed when I see Queen Fannie riding her bike through town. One day, I spotted her, peddling from the direction of Snookey's Tattoo Parlor on Montgomery Street. It's just past Spiegel's

Supermarket and Deli, two doors from Young's Adult Book Store. Only, we call it Young's Nasty Book Store. Queen Fannie was headed in the direction of the Harmony Grove Nursing Home. She visits several times a week. She takes collard greens and other vegetables from her garden, or she volunteers her time by visiting the residents there. She knows everybody very well, especially Mrs. Mattie Johnson, Willie Mae Williams, and Old Man Duffy. I'll tell you about Old Man Duffy some other time. It's kind'f shameful, I can't promise you that I'll tell you everything concerning him. But I can tell you, we like everybody at Harmony Grove, except for him.

Well, anyway, we had just left the Dollar Discount Store. Tiffany had her karaoke recorder turned up to volume ten as we walked down the street singing along to a song by the Supremes when I heard Queen Fannie's bicycle bell. I grabbed Tiffany with one hand and Brianna with the other and pushed them behind a row of tall huckleberry hedges and turned the recorder down real low. I wish you could've seen the surprised looks on my cousins' faces. They looked at me like I had lost my mind until they heard the sound of her bicycle bell, too. Then, we heard her sing, "Hello, my little angels," as she peddled by the bush that I thought had hidden us so well.

You know, Queen Fannie says she feels her best when she smells the earth and a soft breeze blows across her face. She knows that all is well. She had the most perfect look on her face when she peddled *by the bush. Deep down inside of me, I knew she was happy, but we were embarrassed. Well, mostly I was. Dang! How was I to know she had spotted us, too?*

"Silky, come on. I'm ready to go now," Freda said as she impatiently looked up from the banister of their two story colonial home. She glanced at the hardwood floors, taking note that they needed to be sanded and stained in the worst way. She fumbled with the locket around her neck, making sure it was straight. Then, she twisted her diamond tennis bracelet until it felt just right.

Meanwhile, Silky took a last inventory of herself. Smiling, she whispered, "Blue jeans look good. I LOVE SLOAN ELEMENTARY SCHOOL t-shirt looks good. Tennis shoes look good. Braids look exceptional."

Silky shook her head ever so slightly. The colorful beads felt like smooth gems, gliding across her stately nose and high cheekbones. She loved that feeling. She loved what she saw. After she finished primping, she struck a pose just like a model.

The sassy chocolate girl winked, puckered her full lips, and blew a kiss to her reflection. Without a second thought, she knew her cousins would be wearing the same outfit and looking just as good as she did. Before she forgot, Silky hastily opened the top drawer of her oak dresser and took out a pack of blueberry bubble gum that was hidden under her socks. She unwrapped the gum and folded it three times. Then, she shoved the wad of sugary sweet blue stuff into her mouth. She savored the sweet taste of heaven and stashed the rest in her pocket to share with her cousins.

Silky sprung to her feet, and grabbed her sweater. Her long shapely legs moved swiftly down the stairs to reach her mother, who was still standing at the bottom of the landing. After kissing Freda on the cheek, she briskly said, "Hi, Ma." Then, she blew a big blue bubble and said, "Don't I look real neat?" She gestured with both hands, chewing her gum wildly. Silky had a good relationship with Freda. They talked about everything.

"Hi, back at you, honey. You do look real cute. Will you and your cousins be wearing matching outfits again? Oops!? Oh dear, silly me," Freda said, quickly placing her fingers lightly over her mouth. She already knew it was a ridiculous question. Dressing like peas in a pod was a cute little habit the girls had adopted since they were little girls, but the "cute little habit" was getting old because the girls were older now. She looked at how well the jeans fit her growing daughter. Almost like a woman, she thought.

"Silky," Freda said, tugging at the waistband of her daughter's jeans. "You're growing so fast. You might need a larger pant size. They look like they're busting at the seams!"

"Yeah, I'm getting curves just like a woman," Silky said half jokingly while wiggling her hips.

"Silky, please, you're still a child," Freda said with authority.

"I know, Momma, but I am growing," Silky said in a pleading tone.

Suddenly, Freda said, "Wow, child, I'm about to burn up. Did someone touch that thermostat back there?" She glanced toward the hall where the forbidden zone was. She searched for her fan and found it at the bottom of her hand bag. She grabbed it and wildly fanned her pretty face.

"No, Momma, I still have on my toasty sweater. See?" Silky said, buttoning up her cardigan.

"I know you're getting big, sweetie. You're growing hips, and I'm growing gray hair. What a trade off!" She said with playful sarcasm.

"Momma, you know we like to dress alike all the time," Silky seemed to get a personal satisfaction when she explains this to her mother or anyone else even if it's for the umpteenth time. Then, she added, "That's our trademark. We couldn't be best friends if we didn't. I just can't wait to see what kind of pattern we're going to choose for our bridesmaid dresses. Everything has to be exactly the same, you know? What do you think, Ma?" Silky probed.

"What do I think about what, Silky?"

"About us looking like three peas in a pod. That's what Aunt Fannie calls us."

"That's between you, Tiffany, Brianna, and your Aunt Fannie. No matter what you girls wear, you'll still be pretty bridesmaids. Okay, Silky," Freda said, cutting the conversation short. "We need to hurry now." She slid on her oversized sunglasses as Silky looked on. Silky always admired her mother's good looks. When she wore her eyeglasses and accentuated her lips with brown berry lipstick, she thought her mother resembled a movie star. Freda pressed the remote to open the garage door.

"I'm so happy my oldest sister and Neva are finally getting married. They've been courting for a long, long time now. They've been courting before you were even born," she said, reminiscing. "He's a decent man, he owns his own haberdashery business on the boulevard and has for years. He tips his hat when he's in the presence of ladies. I like that, Silky. I like that a lot. That's a sign of a real gentleman. He's a real good catch."

"I know, Momma. You say that all the time."

"Well, your cousins are probably at the fitting already," Freda said as she pulled the seatbelt around her waist. "Oh, my goodness," she thought, she continued pulling more and more to connect it to the other end. With a weary laugh, she said, "Looks like both of us might need everything little larger around the hips, she chuckled. So, is Cool Aid coming to the wedding?" Freda asked as she put the car in first gear.

"I think so. I sent him an invitation. Aunt Fannie said I could," Silky answered hopefully.

"Well, I just hope he gets a haircut. You know how your father feels about boys wearing their hair in braids, after a certain age" her mother responded. There was no response from Silky.

"What were you doing so quietly up in your room, Silky?" Her mother curiously asked with a frown on her face.

"Writing in that diary," Silky responded nonchalantly.

"You mean in the pretty little leopard printed one your Aunt Fannie gave you for your birthday?"

After blowing a bubble, she replied, "But I really wanted the blueberry lip gloss with the nail polish to match. That's what I really wanted, you know? Something I could really treasure."

"Silky, don't be selfish and stop complaining. Be grateful and please get rid of that gum. It's about to drive me crazy," her mother said with waning patience.

"Momma, I'm supposed to be exciting, fresh, and lively 'cause I'm young and almost grown, it's suppose to be the best time of my life!" she said, playfully as she snapped her fingers high in the air. "Writing in a diary doesn't do it for me, but lip gloss does."

"Now, you just calm yourself down, little girl. Whining doesn't become you. A diary is nice. I had one when I was a young girl. There were a lot of precious memories in that little book I had," Freda said defiantly, adjusting the rear view mirror.

"It'll do for the time being," Silky said giving in a little.

Ignoring her daughter's plea, Freda said, "It's about to rain again. Look at those fat dark clouds," Freda pointed as she removed her sunglasses.

"Yeah," Silky said, disappointed.

"I hope your Aunt Fannie doesn't give us any more collards today. We have enough in the freezer to last forever."

"You mean 'bouquet of collards'," Silky giggled, while playfully correcting her mother.

Both Silky and her mother looked at each other and had a good laugh as they drove their little red sports car around the bend and into the busy streets towards the castle on Herbert Way.

Chapter Three

Tiffany

Diary,

I'll going to tell you something that's out of this world Diary, you should see how insane we act when we're really, really happy, I mean we are absolutely happy when we get the key from Queen Fannie to the castle. After school we usually meet outside the school gym, it's located on the closest corner to Herbert Way. Sometimes we try to out run each other there and at other times we'll be giggling and laughing for no reason at all, all the way to the castle. Diary, fun is an insanely good feeling.

Once inside we rush to the top floor, up there is Queen Fannie's Magic Room the most enchanted room in the castle. Since it's up in the attic, it's the closest room to heaven. This is where we fantasize about being famous and glamorous stars. It's the only room in the house where you can truly transform yourself into whoever you want to be. It's a room completely different from the rest of the old house.

See Diary . . . the walls are made from huge mirrors. They reach from the ceiling all the way down to the floor. Big, round Hollywood lights surround the mirrors, making it easy for you to put on your make-up making sure it matches your complexion just right just like movie stars do.

We put on glamorous wigs and apply eye shadow, rouge, and mascara to look even prettier than we already are. We even like to outline our lips with brown eyeliner and then put on red lipstick on top of that, just like Queen Fannie does.

In the middle of the fancy white marble vanity is an assortment of fabulous little bottles with designer perfume inside. We never touch the perfume, but we know Queen Fannie's favorite fragrance is tea rose. She smells like that all the time.

Queen Fannie gave us permission to wear her wigs, but only when we're in the magic room. Most of them are too big for our small heads, but we still look good. She sometimes wears hairpieces to make it look like she has lots of hair. Weaves and wigs of all shapes and colors are everywhere.

When we're there performing, Earl and Pearl perch themselves on Queen Fannie's vanity between the Styrofoam heads and Tiffany's karaoke recorder. Tiffany always manages to grab hold of the microphone first when we sing "Baby Love". I've only been Diana Ross two times in the magic room. TWO TIMES! You talk'n about being selfish, Tiffany is when it comes to performing.

Brianna has never been and she really doesn't care if she's Diana Ross or not. She'd rather read a book about Diana Ross. But she always has fun. We really love being together. See, Diary, we're the same when we enter the magic room. I know Earl and Pearl think we're pretty amazing. And you know what? We are.

"Pinch me," Ruth chuckled and said in disbelief.

"Pinch me," she repeated as her shapely, petite figure stood dwarfed in the middle of the unfinished dream house that she had built by a local construction company.

"Tiffany, you're standing in the formal dining room, dear," she said with a wave, looking down over the balcony.

"Come up here where the bedrooms are. Come see your room. Be careful now. Don't touch the dry walls. They're still wet with spackle," Ruth said, in a muffled tone. She held a hanky over her nose to keep from breathing in the fumes of fresh spackle and new paint that hung heavy in the air. But even through the hanky, you could still hear the excitement in her voice as she stood in what would be her large master suite with a sitting room attached.

Excited, Tiffany ran up the stairs with a wide grin and stood in the space that would be her bedroom. It was twice the size of her old bedroom in the apartment. She was also excited about having her own bathroom. She grinned at her mother and joked, "Yeah, I'm moving up in the world, now all I need now is a daddy." That last statement painfully jabbed at Ruth's heart. So she pretended not to hear Tiffany's cry, yet she knew . . . she knew all too well how desperately her daughter wanted a father.

Tiffany was even excited about the view from her bedroom window. It faced the backyard, overlooking the big hole in the yard. That hole would eventually be the swimming pool, and on the other side of the yard would be the grilling station.

Tiffany was concerned that the new house was on the outskirts of Sloan County, she worried that she might have to transfer to Boone County Elementary School; she didn't want to leave her cousins nor the school she loved.

"Momma, can I have a bay window with a window seat here?" Tiffany asked, pointing with excitement in her eyes. She remembered seeing a window seat in one of the other model houses.

"I hadn't thought about a window seat, but it would be nice, wouldn't it? Ruth stared at the area where Tiffany wanted the window seat, trying to get a feel of what it would be like and said, "even a small shelf over there in the corner for a little lamp would be nice, too, Tiffany. I'll see what I can do if it's not too late. I'm pretty sure the builder would consider it an upgrade though." With a look of concern, she scanned the room with a pressed polished fingernail against her cheek. Ruth gently tried to persuade Tiffany to reconsider the color scheme of her room. Honey she said, "You know mauve is a pretty color too, why don't you think about changing your color scheme to mauve instead of blue? Mauve is such a soothing, peaceful color."

"So is blue," Tiffany said without a second thought.

Ruth sucked her teeth and rolled her eyes up toward the ceiling. Her numerous attempts to change Tiffany's mind had been fruitless. After completing a tour of what would be their new home, the two exited the property and headed towards Ruth's car.

"I have my old lava lamp from the seventies in the trunk of the car. We'll make a stop at Fannie's shop and drop it off. Maybe, she can sell it. It still makes those dreamy blue bubbles," Ruth said as she opened the car door of her late model silver BMW, she waited for Tiffany to buckle her seatbelt.

Ruth was much happier after she finished law school. She had landed a good paying job with Sloan County's successful Martindale, Booker and Styles law firm. This gave her financial relief. Living expenses weren't an issue now; she was able to pay her bills automatically and had plenty of money to spare to go on impromptu shopping sprees in upscale boutiques. She even treated herself to the expensive diamond cocktail ring she had on.

Tiffany was enrolled in the elite Sloan County Music Academy for Gifted Young Voices. Ruth was relieved that the days of singing in the laundry room were over for Tiffany, but she realized that it had been a learning experience for her budding star.

Ruth, however, thought that Tiffany and her cousins should have outgrown dressing in matching outfits by now, but the blood of the Busby family seemed to run stronger than ever in the girls.

Ruth found it lonely raising Tiffany by herself though. Tiffany was a baby when her father died. She put all her energy into raising Tiffany, putting her career on hold and even romance was put on hold. She never remarried, and dated very little but knew a father figure would improve Tiffany's life in other ways.

For a couple of years now Ruth secretly had an eye on Neva's best friend . . . Eli Cunningham. He was always around when there were family gatherings on Herbert Way and he always paid Ruth special attention. Why . . . he was almost like family, and good looking too. Ruth heard he was going to be the best man at Fannie's wedding.

For a long time, Ruth didn't think she could have made such a bold decision to go to law school if it wasn't for the help of her sister-in-laws. Tiffany spent many days, nights and weekends with her cousins when Ruth worked the third shift at the auto plant in town and days attending law school, and week-ends studying. Fortunately, it had worked out well for Tiffany, her life didn't miss a beat, she had all the comforts of home in either house. She had her cousins, it was just like being at home with Brianna or Silky, and her aunts and uncle were just like surrogate parents.

So now the new house would be a new starting point, a new life, for both Ruth and Tiffany. "Okay. Let's hurry and drop off this lamp before we go to the fitting. Who's the new seamstress your Aunt Fannie hired to make the gowns?" Ruth asked.

"I don't know. I haven't met her yet, but I hate that place, Momma," Tiffany blurted out all in one sentence. As she sat on the passenger side, she nervously took the rubber band out of her long straight pony tail. Then, she carefully pulled the loose strains back together again and put the rubber band back on, pouting all the while.

"Can I stay in the car while you go in, please, Ma?" She implored with her eyes squeezed together and her hands in the praying position, just like a little girl.

"No, you can't stay in the car. What are you talking about Tiffany you have to go inside and speak to Hazel. She's most likely there watching the shop. All you have to do is say hi. You don't have to say another word. Don't ever use the word hate, and don't stare; just smile. Be kind, Tiffany. She's a lonely, wonderful old woman who loves you," she said in a soft but stern voice.

"Ma, I really feel like I want to puke every time I go into that store. It's like a creepy dungeon from the dark ages. There's too much junk around. Besides, I always see Hazel's mouth moving, even when she's the only one in the shop!"

"Can't you find a better word than puke, Tiffany?"

"Okay, throw-up," she said, sarcastically throwing her arms in the air. Then, she continued her ranting, "I can't help it, Momma. It smells like Harmony Grove, you know? Even Aunt Fannie's house reminds me of that shop. Humph, all those old pictures of dead folks hanging around the house. They give me the creeps."

"This is an antique shop. I have you know that antiques are big business nowadays. Your Aunt Fannie makes a decent living selling antiques. So, think before you turn your nose up, little girl. Besides, Hazel loves you and your cousins. She's known y'all since you were born, so show some respect. She's like family," Ruth scolded.

"Ugh! Ma, she's a creepy little woman who's even weirder than Aunt Fannie and her collard greens. You'll see, just don't take your eyes off her," Tiffany responded, sweeping loose strands of hair behind her ears.

"And you remember what I told you, Tiffany. Your Aunt Fannie isn't weird. She's just eccentric, and so is Hazel.

They've been like that forever. It's nothing new to the people in town. They're comfortable with their peculiar ways. Now, hush. Enough of this crazy talk, you and your cousins have wild imaginations. You girls should write for Disney Studios. You'd make a bundle of money," Ruth said sarcastically as she pulled up in front of the small well kept antique shop. Secretly, Ruth and Freda had always thought Hazel was a little odd, so she added with a short laugh, "But you're right about the collard greens, dear. It has gotten out of control."

A bright light in the dark front window flashed OPEN in large red blocked letters. Ruth stepped down the two steps and opened the door. A piercing cowbell ringed as Tiffany walked in behind her mother.

"Hello," Ruth sang, looking for signs of life. She didn't see Hazel, but she did see a lot of everything else that cluttered the walls and crammed the dusty corners. So much stuff hung from the ceiling because floor space was at a premium. Tiffany left the door behind her ajar in case she needed to make a quick escape.

Tiffany spotted Hazel sitting at a table with a gruesome looking life sized clown. Her mouth was moving, and her eyes were smiling. She appeared to be having a conversation with the clown.

"Hello, there," she finally said happily in her raspy voice, but Ruth couldn't tell where the voice was coming from.

"Hazel, is that you, where are you?" Ruth asked apprehensively. Her forehead had begun to glisten with sweat. Her daughter's warnings were fresh in her mind. Ruth's heart started to pound her eyes began to get larger, darting from one corner to the other.

Holding her breath and trying not to smell, Tiffany suspiciously stepped back. She waved her pale right hand behind her, feeling for the door knob.

"Here I am, darlings, sitting at this stunning Henry the Fifth mahogany table, underneath the large crystal chandelier that once graced the Cathedral of St. John of England, right in front of you. Here, dear, here," she directed while smiling, waving her long white arm with flab waving back.

Tiffany immediately focused on Hazel's white Afro, which oddly enough, the girls swear it looked like a small piece of white cloud landed on her head and never left. Hazel was the only white person the girls had ever seen with an afro. It still amazed them to this day.

Indeed, there she was amongst the cluttered junk. She and the gruesome looking clown blended in so well.

Chapter Four

Brianna

Diary,

I'm writing from underneath my bed covers 'cause I'm grounded and not allowed to turn the lights on in my own room. It's a good thing I still have my daddy's flashlight from the garage, so I can see what I need to see. Diary, that disrespectful Camisha Tolbertson got me in trouble again. See, it's like this.

Ms. Thunder told Camisha to spit out her gum. Camisha put up a big fuss 'cause it was still juicy and full of flavor. She wasn't ready to give up that goodness without a few fighting words. She cut a mean eye at Ms. Thunder while stomping to the back where the trash can was. Then, she yelled, "OKAY, MS. THUNDERBUTT, YOU GET ON MY LAST NERVE!" Then she spit her gum out.

"Ms. Thunderbutt," I yelled and laughed real hard, and real loud. I couldn't believe Camisha had the nerve to call her that. I was totally out of control, my loose leaf book and Social Studies papers fell all over the floor. Real tears fell out of my eyes. I held onto my stomach 'cause it ached from laughing so hard. I didn't realize I was the only one in the classroom laughing, though. I felt foolish when I calmed down, but it was too late to clean up my act 'cause the entire class was glaring at me, even Ms. Thunder, waited for me to get my act together.

Me and Camisha were sent to detention for the rest of the day. Ms. Thunder called our mothers. My momma grounded me for two whole days for actin' the fool in class. Luckily, I can still write real good underneath these covers.

Have I told you about Cool Aid my heart throb? His real name isn't Cool Aid though; it's Kadeem Jackson, and he's real cute. He looks a little like Denzel, you know, the actor. See, he's the only boy I like to exchange homework with 'cause he's super smart, like me. Both of us made the honor roll this year. He can even say his nine timetables backwards. That's just too cool, but my daddy's not impressed..

He doesn't think Cool Aid is as terrific as I think he is, but my daddy doesn't have a clue. He freaked out when he saw Cool Aid's braids, and he thinks Cool Aid walks like a pimp, but he doesn't understand. Just because Cool Aid sways when he walks doesn't mean he's trying to pimp walk. He was born to walk like that!

My daddy has totally forgotten that he wore an afro when he was growing up, and that was a big thing then. Grown-ups seem to forget that they went through a militant period back in the day. Speaking of periods, I haven't experienced that magic moment yet, I'm not worried though . . . that subject just popped into my head. Wow that was weird!

Well anyway, I have a picture of my daddy from when he was in college. He was on the football team. In the picture, he had just taken off his helmet, but his afro didn't know because it kept the same shape as the helmet! Me and my cousins laugh all the time when we see that picture. We call it the "helmet hairdo."

I always say, "Daddy, did I tell you that Cool Aid is the undisputed oratorical winner two years in a row at school?" He just ignores the good parts about my Cool Aid.

Daddy always asks, "Has Kadeem gotten a haircut, yet?" or "Has Kadeem ventured into a barber shop lately?" It's the only time my daddy mentions his name. Daddy always calls him by his birth name, too, all proper like. Never Cool Aid.

Daddy just stubbornly sits in his big recliner and talks from behind the sports section of the Sloan Daily. He's out of touch with everything that's real, especially important things like this 'cause he doesn't realize that Cool Aid is the sugar in my bubble gum.♥

"Ma, you know Mr. Old Man Duffy?" Brianna asked in a small hesitant voice.

"You mean sweet Mr. Duffy, the one in the wheelchair at Harmony Grove Nursing Home?"

"Yeah, ma . . . him, but he's not so sweet as he pretends to be. I've wanted to tell you," she said with her head down, looking at her shoes. By this time, Mable sensed something was wrong.

"What?" She asked, wide-eyed and anxious.

"Instead of calling me and my cousins by our real names, he gave us pet names. He calls Silky 'Chocolate Chip' because she's the darkest of us three. He calls Tiffany, 'Vanilla' because she's the lightest, and um . . . he calls me 'Olive Oil' because I'm brown and on the thin side. Ma, we don't like being called names because he's more into what makes us different than what makes us a-like. We try to duck him every time we visit Harmony Grove, but he wheels around in his wheelchair with a big smile on his face and thick, thick glasses on until he finds us."

Mable glanced back at her daughter and said, "Well, Brianna, they sound like names of endearment to me, but he should call you by your real names, if that's what you girls want. I don't think he means any harm, so think on the positive side, baby girl. Don't be on the defensive. If it bothers you girls that much, tell him you'd much rather he called you by the names you were born with. That's all."

Mable paused again, searching for a reasonable explanation other than the complexion thing her daughter had alluded to. She couldn't figure it out, she realized though that people could be mean and hurtful sometimes, but not sweet Mr. Duffy. He's probably forgotten their names. "He might be in the early stages of dementia," she murmured to herself.

"Sometimes, you have to forgive people and move on, Brianna. Don't get yourself all worked up about it, but you're right, being old doesn't give him the right to give you girl's pet names if you don't like it. On the other hand, if he really hasn't forgotten your real names, then that's being rude. So, one of you girls should tell him politely, and I do mean politely, Brianna. Be diplomatic and respect your elders, okay?" she said with some concern.

There was a long silence. Worried Brianna wanted to tell her mother something else but she dismissed the thought. She was much too embarrassed to talk about it so she changed the subject. Besides, she knew that Silky didn't want anyone to know. Both she and Tiffany promised not to tell anyone, so instead Brianna asked, "Momma, when can I go to Chicago to see my daddy? I miss him."

Mable took a while before she answered. She realized that she too missed her husband. It was hard being by herself. She didn't like it but never told anyone how she really felt being without her husband.

"Well, Thanksgiving is coming up. Call your father and see if he can arrange for you to spend that long weekend with him."

"Oh, goody," Brianna said with an exuberance she hadn't shown since she had started her period. She suddenly realized that it meant that she and her mother would not be together for one of the most important holidays of the year. Brianna looked at her mother with her big brown eyes and whined, "But that means I won't be with you for Thanksgiving, Momma."

Mable sighed heavily before she answered, thinking all the while. "Yes, that's right, dear, our first important holiday apart."

"Ma, is Daddy ever coming home to live with us again?"

"I don't know, sweetie."

"Why? Are you and daddy still mad at each other? Why aren't we a family like before? Things aren't good without daddy and Thanksgiving isn't going to be good without you."

"It's not that things are not good, they're just not the same."

"Do you hate him, Momma?" Brianna probed.

"No, darling, we might get back together. We just need our space for now."

"But we're supposed to be a family, and we should share the same space together. Tiffany wants a daddy real bad and I want my daddy back home with us. Silky is the only one with a real daddy, she's the lucky one."

"Never mind, Brianna, let's talk about something pleasant," Mable said, grabbing for a large paper towel from the kitchen counter and wiping the sweat from around her neck.

"Maybe he'll come back, and we can share our space again," Mable said with an air of appeasement. She hoped that the truth wouldn't upset her daughter too much. She didn't think her Ned would ever come back to live with them.

Brianna looked down at the white tiling on the kitchen floor, trying to make sense of her confusion. Deep sadness overwhelmed her as she thought of not having her father home to hug whenever she needed a hug. She loved her father and wanted everything perfect just like it used to be.

Both men in Brianna's life, whom she loved dearly, her brother Jabari and her dad, lived in other states now. It was just Brianna and her mother, an incomplete family according to Brianna. It too was a difficult situation for Mable to bear, the feeling of incompleteness tore at her everyday. She truly missed her Ned.

"We have two errands to make before we head on over to Herbert Way. We'll go to Harmony Grove to drop off these collards, then we'll swing over to the post office and mail Jabari's care box. We only have a little time to spare okay, sweetie?" Mable said as she bent over, showing her very big bottom while searching in her freezer, taking out three large plastic bags of collard greens. Mable was the only sister who wore her hair in a short natural style showing off her sprinkling of gray. She believed that she had earned her crown of gray hair. It was her tribute to a life well lived.

"Momma, you're giving away some more collard greens?"

"Why not, dear, there are more people at Harmony Grove than just the two of us. Fannie's garden is wonderful indeed; she can feed the entire neighborhood. I just hope she doesn't give us any more of these greens."

"Poor Fannie, I really think she's losing it. I don't think either her or Hazel are playing with a full deck. Hump, hump, hump," she said, shaking her head slowly from side to side. She continued, "It's funny how life turns the tables. When we were growing up, Fannie was the very one who took care of your Aunt Freda, your Uncle Jimmy, and me. Daddy worked them long hard overtime hours, as a mail man, and Dear did day work on the other side town. Now, I just don't know anymore. I don't know," she said sadly.

"Aunt Ruth calls them eccentric. We don't mind that our Aunt Fannie's weird," Brianna said sweetly. Forcing a smile, she said, "She's just a little different, Ma. She's a lot of fun though, especially when she jumps rope with us. Then, there was the time she taught us how to play old maids. We have a real good time when she gives us permission to play dress up in her fancy clothes in the magic room. Besides, Aunt Fannie's hands come in handy as the fourth pair when we play Ms. Mary Mac."

"Well, I don't know about all that. I think she's off her rocker particularly when it comes down to these darn collard greens and that second hand store she calls an antique shop, ugh."

"Do we have to go inside Harmony Grove? We're gonna be late for the fitting. Besides, my cousins are probably already there," she said as they got into their two-year-old white SUV.

"Just for a minute, dear, I want to drop off these greens."

Mable briefly looked up at the gray sky and thought about her handsome eighteen-year-old son away at college.

Breaking the silence, Mable said, "By the way, how is my big girl feeling today? Is your stomach cramping much?"

"No, and don't tell anyone, okay, Momma? You promise?"

"Don't worry, dear. I won't say a word. It's good you don't have cramps, I used to take aspirins to keep from cramping all the time," Mable said in an upbeat tone.

"Is Jabari coming to the wedding?" Brianna asked. Her mood brightened up when she changed the conversation to her brother.

"Brianna, you talk to your brother more than I do. You should know. In fact, I should be asking you. I suggest you call your brother this evening. I don't know if your father will be able to make it. He mentioned something about a business trip."

"I know," Brianna whimpered.

It started to rain hard. Mable was lucky to find a parking space a few yards away from the entrance to the post office.

Brianna grabbed the box while her mother grabbed the umbrella from the back seat. As they walked together in the rain in silence, Mable tried to comfort her daughter by gently hugging her close. Brianna pulled away and lagged behind her mother allowing the rain to mix with her tears.

Chapter Five

The Welcoming Committee

Diary,

It's raining. It rained yesterday and the day before that.

I'm bored, so I'll write about something funny, okay? Dairy, this happened about two years ago, but I can remember it like it was yesterday, when me and my cousins were dressing up in Queen Fannie's party clothes in the room-sized closet next to the magic room.

Now, I got to let you know, we were young and not very smart! Now that I am twelve years old and know a lot more, I can't imagine how immature we were.

Well, it's like this, the attic was one big dark room until Queen Fannie had the room separated. One part is pretty, light, and airy. We call that room "the magic room". The other part is old, untouched, and kind of spooky. Well, that was the part of the attic we were in that day.

I remember being on my tippy toes when I pulled the long string which turned on the dim light blub. It was bright enough to see most things, especially the cobwebs.

Brianna mysteriously disappeared all the way to the back. Behind the colorful dresses, where three racks of dusty, old coats hung.

You could see rows and rows of beautiful satin and silk dresses. These were clothes fit for a queen. Some of them were long, and some of them were short, but all of them were fancy as far as our eyes could see. Tons of shoes were kept in the same old shoe boxes that they were bought in, and some were simply stored on built-in metal shelves. There was a large dusty credenza that had thick dust on top and cobwebs on the knobs of the drawers. Stored in the corner were five round flowered cardboard boxes protecting the Queen's old hats.

We've never seen our Queen Fannie with any of this stuff on before. Anyway, I tried on a flashy pinstriped purple and gold satin dress. It was long. It touched the floor, and it almost fit me. Well, sort of.

Anyway, Tiffany managed to untie a tight knot that kept a hat inside the box. She took the top off and took out a red, wide brimmed hat wrapped in old, thin tissue paper. It was one of those hats you would hate to sit behind if a lady had it on in church. Besides being fiery red, it had a long, fluffy red feather on the side that swept to the back.

Underneath the hat was a furry b-o-a (I think that's what my Momma calls it). It was made from ostrich feathers that had been dyed red. Tiffany wrapped it around her neck three times, and it still dragged the floor. She put the hat on and tilted it over her left eye. With her brown hair hanging over her shoulders, I almost forgot she was my real blood cousin. She looked just like a movie star. We laughed as I kicked off my gym shoes and pulled off my socks, slipping my bare feet into a pair of purple stilettos. They matched the dress perfectly. We loved playing and acting like grown women.

Tiffany found a wooden rectangular box underneath a separate sheet of tissue paper. Oh, it was such a pretty brown smooth, box and it looked brand new, not all dusty like the rest of the stuff in the attic. I told Tiffany to open the box, so she did. In there were tight rows of cigars wrapped in their own individual cellophane wrappers. Tucked along the lining was a small book of matches. On the top flap was a faded advertisement for Lucky Strike cigarettes. Tiffany decided to rip the wrapper off one of the cigars.

At first, we marveled at the bigness of the cigar and the golden paper ring around it that spelled funny words I had never seen before: VegaFine Robusto. We thought the small writing spoiled the usefulness of the ring for some reason. We kept it on. We didn't care if it got burned up 'cause we were about to smoke that bad boy. It would be our first cigar ever! Tiffany quietly struck a small match on the striking pad. After a couple of tries,—Poof!—a tiny yellow spark appeared and changed into a small pyramid of swaying friendly fire. At first, we just glared at it. Then, I took a couple of puffs to get it burning just right. Suddenly, we heard Queen Fannie calling from below in an almost frantic voice, asking us if we smelled smoke. Of course, both of us lied and yelled back, "No!" We waited a few minutes to see if she would come up the stairs. She didn't. We still didn't know where Brianna was, but Tiffany took a long puff from the cigar. I quickly told her, "Don't inhale." But dang, it was said too late. She inhaled, and her pretty face turned as red as Elmo. Her eyes filled with a lot of tears, and she began coughing non stop. I grabbed the cigar out of her hand and stabbed the friendly fire part out with my stilettos.

I snatched the hat off her head and began fanning her until her natural pale color came back. I pounded her on the back until she stopped coughing. I could tell she was almost back to normal by the way she grabbed the hat out of my hand and slapped it back on her head. I put my hand on my hip and quietly told her off. "I told you not to inhale, you'll get us in trouble girl."

Me and Tiffany almost had a fallen out, but when Tiffany opened her mouth to defend herself a hiccup came out instead. Then, another one came popping out, and then another. She couldn't speak a single word 'cause she was having a hiccup fit. I was so mad 'cause she was spoiling our fun. That was supposed to be fun time. I told that silly girl not to inhale, and wanted to know where Brianna was when I needed her?

Well, while I was cleaning up the ashes, you know who finally came sashaying back from who knows where with a happy grin on her face. She calmly said, "What's the matter with you, Tiffany?" But she didn't wait for an answer. Instead, she said, "Look at this amazing coat I found in the back of the coat rack."

This kind's "fun" was wrack'n my nerves. I got nauseous watching Brianna twirling around and around and around like a crazed ballerina, modeling that ugly coat. I got a good look at it, though. It had a weird lookin' reddish brown fur for a collar.

Frowning, Tiffany pushed the hat away from her eyes to get a better look at the fur. Her frown worried me when she murmured, "That's an ugly looking piece of mink fur."

I whispered, "Yeah."

That was when I noticed Tiffany's hiccups were cured, but I also noticed that her smile was gone too. Brianna honestly believed she was lookin' as good as me and Tiffany.

We leaned over a little bit closer to get a better look at the mangy lookin' thing, and it looked back at us with black beady little eyes. It had the smell of strong moth balls. It even had grimy little toes with claws. It was simply disgusting. We held our nose and looked at it like it was something out of a horror show!! Brianna stared into our frightened faces and sensed something was terribly wrong. She began to struggle to unfasten the grizzly coat's button from underneath her chin. While she was struggling, I knew without a doubt that I saw the cunning movement of that creature's head. It's mouth cracked wide open showing a snarly sneer of razor sharp teeth. "Ooowee" that was just too much for me to take in, before I could let out a scream, Tiffany beat me to it, pointing and yelling, at the top of her lungs. "Oh, snap! It's a rat! No, it's a giant rodent! Brianna had a giant rodent around her pretty neck."

Scared to death, Brianna jumped up and down and managed to unfasten the coat and flipped it off her shoulders. Without a second thought she began screaming along with us while at the same time she was trying to wipe the skin off of her neck with both hands. All three of us screamed just like we were in a Hollywood horror movie; only this was for real. We flew down the stairs and into the kitchen where Queen Fannie was, it was safe there. I was so scared diary, that I didn't even feel those seventeen steps under my feet. I know that there are seventeen because I count them every time I go up to the magic room. And check this out; I didn't even realize that I still had Queen Fannie's stilettos on! I must have sprouted wings and glided down those stairs.

Before I knew it, we were standing in front of Queen Fannie where she had been sipping her herb tea and enjoying her solitude. We knew she had heard all the noise 'cause her hand was shaking as she sat her teacup down in the saucer to see what the commotion was all about. She looked up with a frown from her pretty made up face as she grabbed her gold-rimmed eyeglasses.

"What's all the to-do about, girls?" she asked in a stern voice.

Wide eyed and out of breath, Tiffany and I pointed to Brianna and yelled, "Brianna had a giant, weird looking rat around her neck."

"A weird looking what?" Queen Fannie asked, confused and worried.

"A rat," I yelled. "No some kind of a rodent!"

Tiffany's eyes were popped out. She was shaking real hard, and all she could say was "Yeah . . . yeah."

"Yeah, it was hanging on the back of the black wool coat that Brianna had on," I said, excited and out of breath, and it smelled disgusting."

Brianna just stood there, shaken, teary-eyed, and feeling totally ri-dic-u-lous. I don't think Brianna had even seen the creature, but she definitely saw the bear in our faces. That's why she ran for her life, too!

Anyway, Queen Fannie thought for a moment. Then, a little smile came over her pretty red lips. She said she knew what coat we were talking about. It was the coat with Dear's red fox pelt attached for decoration and style. Then she tried to correct the way Brianna had it on she said, it hung from the shoulder and not the back, sweetie. Then in a cheerful voice she said, "Isn't that a wonderful wool coat? I wore it a few times with your Uncle Schine when we started dating. It used to be the style back in the day. It used to be hip. You know, angels, that was the style," she said, trying to convince us that it was okay.

"Hip?" I asked sarcastically

I thought it sounded crazy! Now come on, Diary. Am I missing something here? It doesn't make a bit of sense. What were adults thinking about "back in the day?" All three of us looked at each other and wondered how could someone wear a dead fox with the black beady eyes and grungy toes dangling from her shoulder. How could that be hip? It even had those snarly daggers hanging out of its mouth . . . Oh lawd, what a frightful sight that was!

This was the very first time we've seen the Queen on the spot. She was sweating with a dopey look on her face, fumbling for a better answer.

She said, "At that time, people weren't as aware as they are today about endangered animals and all. Now, many of us realize how foolish it was." Then, she said, "I know my precious angels would understand!"

See Dairy! Our Queen is cool like that. She tuned us out and continued sipping her herb tea. We didn't say another word about that old coat 'cause we loved her too much to keep her on the spot. Brianna learned her lesson. She never ever went into the back of that closet again.

Between the short flashes of sunshine, dark swollen clouds rolled in, cooling down the muggy September afternoon. A peaceful downpour moved in swiftly. It stopped just as fast as it started.

Chapter Five The Welcoming Committee

As they approached Fannie's house, Silky saw the four large cypress trees that framed the lavish landscaping that began at the foot of the hill. The trees had been seedlings when her mother was a young girl. Each sibling had planted one when they were children. Over the years, the trees had grown tall, and mature like uniformed guards. They protected the house, providing year round shade and a safe haven for neighborhood birds.

Grand entryways, collard greens, and antiques were important to Fannie. She never worried much about the roof that needed mending or the bricks that were missing from the sides of the house. The railings were also missing a few spindles, and the ones that were there could use a fresh coat of paint. The old house was in need of repair, but Fannie only saw the need for a new front door. In fact, she had the outdated door replaced ten years ago along with the screen door. She replaced them with two massive oak doors and painted the doors bright red. What made the doors so magnificent was the elaborately designed stained glass panels that started midway the door and ended at the top where the arch began. They were beautiful panels of colorful leaves and flowers all surrounding the motif of a large peacock's head with dazzling feathers. It gave the old brick house the look of prominence, welcoming guests and unexpected peddlers in a most grandiose way.

She liked the doors so much that the very same year she had the old rectangle window up in the magic room replaced with an arch-shaped window with the same peacock motif.

The gold tone antique doorknob was larger than any doorknob around town, except for the one on the door of the First Bank of Sloan County and the library two blocks over.

As you drive by the property, you'll have to glance real fast, to catch a glimpse of the porch. That's where Silky took her first steps when she was a toddler. It wrapped around to the back of the house that's where the vegetable garden is located.

Although Fannie's two-acre vegetable garden had seen better days, her collard greens always appeared to be healthier than any other vegetable in her garden. Magically, the clusters of large, emerald green leaves faced upwards, always prepared to enjoy the rich nourishment of the rain and the hot rays from the sun.

As Silky and her mother pulled up in front of the house, Freda noticed Mable's white SUV parked at the muddy curve. Ruth's silver BMW was parked alongside the tall evergreens. There was a fancy, dark green utility vehicle with darkly tinted windows parked in the driveway up close to where Fannie's bike and bike stand were.

Tiffany popped out of the front door upon hearing the distinct sound of the red two-seater sports car. Tiffany's ponytail swung back and forth as she ran to greet Silky and her Aunt Freda.

Immediately, the two girls began jumping up and down, holding on to each others' shoulders, as if they hadn't been in each other's company in years. Their display of affection always amazed Freda.

Tiffany is a pretty girl, a little big, but a pretty girl, Freda thought. And she has such a pleasant personality. She's a lovely young lady indeed. She's a Busby girl just like my baby.

Tiffany's I LOVE SLOAN ELEMENTARY SCHOOL t-shirt was a tad tight, showing off her developing bust line.

Tiffany was coy about the difference between her and her cousin's clothes sizes. She hated going over to the larger sized clothes when she and her cousins went to the mall. She even looked a little more mature than Silky and Brianna did, but just a little.

Seconds later, Brianna came running up, jumping over a puddle in her neatly pressed jeans. She had a hint of red in her almond brown complexion that she had inherited from her father. The wind blew her long wavy hair further away from her lovely face, revealing the fine dark baby hair that laid softly around her forehead and traveled to the nap of her neck, bejeweling her combination of Native American and African American features. Another gust of wind blew, pressing the I LOVE-SLOAN ELEMENTARY SCHOOL t-shirt close to her chest, showing a small set of budding breasts. Freda affectionately thought of "speed bumps" and shamefully laughed to herself.

Freda knew that little Brianna wouldn't be the smallest much longer. It was only a matter of time before she matured into a beautiful young lady.

Yep, thought Freda. There's definitely Busby blood in those veins, too.

Just for a second, Freda thought about Mable and Ned not being together. It briefly interfered with her joy, but only for a second. She didn't allow it to disturb this exceptional moment of love in action. The girls were complete when Brianna joined her cousins in the hugging huddle of love.

Freda marveled as she watched her daughter and nieces touch palms, sharing high fives and giggling their way through Fannie's fancy doors that welcomed everybody. Freda made her way behind the girls, observing their happiness. It reminded her of her own happiness when she, Fannie, Mable, and James were growing up here on Herbert Way, enjoying family, enjoying life.

Chapter Six

Liberating Experience

Diary,

Guess what? I just found out that Brianna got her period the other day, and I still haven't started mine yet! I'm not jealous, but I think I should have been the first to get my period since I'm the oldest. It was my inner child who was jealous, not me.

Me and Momma already talked about periods. I told her everything I had heard about it at school and summer camp, and she told me what was true and what wasn't. Mother Nature has some nerve, making your first time a total surprise. There is no warning or nothing. And the twenty-eight day calendar count is as useful as the sundial. It's the stupidest thing I've ever heard of. It sounds like a trap for disaster, if you ask me.

Brianna was lucky it started while she was at home. Now, I've heard about a lot of scary situations that some of my friends at school have experienced when they got their periods for the very first time. Tamara Wilson, a girl from chorus, got hers at the beach over the summer break. She said she cried all the way to the locker room, holding a towel tightly around her like it was her second skin.

Camisha Tolbertson got hers in P.E. I'm scared to death at the thought of not being prepared. So, you want know what I do to protect myself when that magic moment gets here, Diary? I took one of those old-fashioned pads from my Momma's bathroom and put it in a plastic sandwich bag. That's right. I keep that plastic bag in my denim purse along with a pack of blueberry gum, 2 pencils, a love note from Cool Aid, a picture of me, a dark brown lip liner, a bag of hot fries, $2.35, and two balls of toilet tissue. All of this is in my purse and it's safely tucked in my back pack between my beginners' algebra and English lit text books. I carried it with me everywhere I go, so I was prepared for that tragic moment . . . I mean magic moment. But I'm not nearly as prepared as Tiffany. Since she got her designer lunch box, she stuffs it with her most precious items and carries it every day. But I'm not jealous of her either, especially not that designer lunch box!

I remember asking my Momma if female ants and roaches get periods, too? She didn't answer me. Either the question was too stupid, or she didn't know, but she did say every female gets a period!

To be honest, I was secretly jealous when Brianna finally told us. Me and Tiffany already knew, we just waited for her to fess up. She is supposed to be our best friend.

Chapter Six Liberating Experience

We didn't let on how we found out and I didn't let on how I really felt, but my heart did fall straight down to my naked toenails when she confirmed the rumor.

While we were sitting at the headquarters, nosy Tiffany whispered in a real low voice, like somebody else was around besides us, "Oh, that's wonderful, Brianna, I mean about your period and all. You know what I mean."

Did I say Ms. Hazel was the nut??? Even though she was acting dingy, Tiffany was dead serious. I asked her if she lost her mind. Then, I said, "What's so wonderful about a period? It sounds scary to me?"

Tiffany shushed me and quickly turned back to Brianna. Her ponytail barely missed the tip of my nose. All the while, Diary, I tried not to show that I was all ears, too.

Tiffany asked more stupid questions like "does it hurt?", but I didn't ask anything. My mouth was closed!

"That's definitely too cool, Brianna. It's the sign of being a real woman," Tiffany said.

I said, "Excuse me," with my serious face.

Dairy, I don't understand why Tiffany acted like Brianna had hit the lottery or somethin'. Then, Brianna started to believe what Tiffany was saying. A big smile grew on her face. Then, she said, "Tiffany's right. I am a woman now. Don't you see, Silky?"

Diary, then I realized it was me who was jealous and not my inner child.

"Uh, I don't think so," I said.

"If you ask me, it sounds like the fun of being a kid has been taken away." I thought she was stretching it a bit, too. I mean the point about being a woman and all.

"Well, at the very least Silky, I am a young lady!" she said.

See, I knew my serious face would bring her back down to earth, for real. Now, Diary, you know I was supposed to be the first one to get her period. What did I do wrong? I'm the oldest, so I should have been first, right?

Well, anyway, at least, I was the first to wear a padded training bra!

Ruth playfully greeted Freda and Silky at the door by saying, "Oh, you finally made it, as she briskly, walked towards them, carrying a platter of finger sandwiches Fannie had prepared earlier.

"Yes, we sure did. What time is it?" Freda asked, taking off her light weight jacket.

"It is 12:56", Ruth said after glancing at her watch.

"Wow! Just in time. So, how's my favorite attorney doing?" She gave Ruth a hug. Ruth smelled like collard greens and sweet blueberry muffins.

"I'm doing well. I'm doing well," Ruth said as she hugged Freda back. She placed the platter down next to the red punch and freshly baked blueberry muffins.

"How's the new house coming along?" Freda asked.

"It's coming along, slowly but surely. We can't wait 'til it's finished. Tiffany and I were just over there," she said, holding onto a flowered dishtowel.

Mable walked in from the kitchen and behind her came Fannie, walking briskly. Fannie had one hand in an oven mitt, and the other held a blue and white dishtowel with a colorful drawing of a hen in the middle. She placed a crystal bowl full of hot steamy collard greens in the center of the serving table right next to the finger sandwiches, punch, and blueberry muffins. Then, she greeted her sister and niece each with a big hug. Afterwards, she placed a large serving spoon right beside the main dish. She greeted Silky by saying, "Well, Miss Silky Blue, it looks like you have put on a pound or two."

"Umm . . . my jeans are much tighter around the hips," she said happily with both hands on her hips.

Fannie's flawless brown skin began to show signs of perspiration on her freshly made up face, yet she maintained a dignified air. Even Freda noticed how pretty her sister looked with that four carat engagement ring on her finger.

Now, what is her secret? Could it be because she's getting married? Freda thought. Maybe it's the short blonde pageboy wig she has on. It can't be the greens making her look so radiant, she concluded.

"Help yourself to a plate of greens," Fannie said to no one in particular. "It's good for what ails you, and it makes your skin pretty. Just look at my pretty little angels." The three girls smiled like Cheshire cats.

Over her leopard printed jumpsuit, Fannie wore a small white apron tied tightly around her dainty waistline.

Indeed, Fannie's smooth, silky brown skin was a living testimony to the benefits of collard greens, or so she claimed. Her sisters and sister-in-law weren't convinced, and they didn't return the smile either. The girls promptly helped themselves to generous plates of greens and blueberry muffins. Not that they were delighted to do so, they were just protective of their Aunt Fannie's feelings.

"Oh no," Mable complained with an angry glare in her eyes, "We've had enough collard greens. We have tons of the stuff in our freezer at home already."

To make her point, Mable started counting the number of times on her fingers. "We eat them for lunch. We eat them for dinner. For crying out loud, I've even seen Brianna heat up a side bowl of greens with her blueberry pancakes in the morning. Enough already!"

Mable toned down her attitude a little and softly said, "Everything in moderation, sister dear, everything in moderation, okay, sweetie?"

She forced a smile. Then, she continued, "There are plenty of other vegetables in the garden beside collard greens. There's okra, squash, and green beans!"

The other women in the room silently agreed with Mable, but didn't get into the disagreement they politely stayed out of the fray. The cousins however, looked at each other and chimed in simultaneously with the weirdest looks on their faces, "But we love collard greens."

Tiffany boasted, "And they're not fattening either. They're just perfect for me. Look! I've lost weight." She said putting her hands on her wide hips.

"And they're good for what ails you," Silky said echoing one of Fannie's favorite phases, while scooping up a forkful and shoving it into her mouth.

Fannie was proud of her nieces but was stunned by Mable's rude comments. "Oh, Mable that's a lot of hogwash," She said with a quick wave dismissing Mable's offensive comments.

Confused and speechless, Freda just frowned and shook her head slowly from side to side in quiet protest as she thought to herself, As usual, these girls love their Aunt Fannie. They'll side with her until the ocean turns to a heap of sand.

Meanwhile, Ruth reached for another finger sandwich, raving, "I declare, Fannie, these are mighty tasty hors d'oeuvres." She said nibbling like a bird. Then she settled down with a glass of punch and asked, "Where's Mrs. Crump?"

"I'm coming," a gentle voice said in between two short coughs. They barely heard her soft voice above the loud creaking of the stairs before they saw the big woman emerge from the area of the magic room. She carried a thick pattern book secured under one arm and a tape measure draped around her wide neck. There were three blue swatches between her fingers. One was a light chiffon fabric. The other was a silk blend, and the last was a poly crepe. These were the finest fabrics the girls had ever seen.

Mrs. Crump was a large light-skinned woman with heavily drawn dark eyebrows and bags under her eyes. Deep creases extended from the bottom of her rather wide nostrils to the ends of her big red lips. Her thick black-rimmed glasses had the oddest shape. The ends extended up into a point and were decorated with rhinestones. Her silver and black hair was twisted into a tightly secured bun. A barely noticeable hair net kept it neat and tidy. The large rhinestone brooch pinned between her bosom made her green and brown paisley dress appear dressier than it really was. She reminded the girls of Mrs. Matthews, the school librarian.

"Gosh, she must have made a gazillion dresses in her day," Brianna whispered out loud. Mrs. Crump had a stern, no nonsense manner about her. She didn't smile. She didn't terry about. She was all about business, in a military sort of way. She certainly didn't match that fancy new utility vehicle that was parked in Fannie's driveway. It had to be hers.

What a strange looking woman. I wonder where Fannie knows her from, thought Mable. She knew it was bad manners to stare, but she couldn't figure her out. Was Crump a French or Mexican surname? Mable tried desperately to look at something else, like the girls choking down collard greens or Fannie tossing her head about, but her eyes seemed to float back to Mrs. Crump and her unusually large hands. She glanced at the way they gripped the swatches of fine chiffon and silk blend fabrics. Mable was sure the fabrics would be permanently creased.

"Come. Sit a spell and take a load off your feet," Mable tactfully offered, moving her hips over to make room on Fannie's pea green Duncan Phyfe sofa. Mrs. Crump didn't say a word. She just waved her hand, rejecting the offer. She proceeded to walk to the cluttered coffee table. Clearing a spot, she laid the large pattern book down. The women in the room couldn't help but notice the black thick-heeled orthopedic shoes Mrs. Crump had on.

Poor woman, those comfort shoes must be hot and uncomfortable, Mable thought.

The silence in the room was deafening. Family members glanced around with wide leery eyes along with bated breath they waited for the girls' reaction. Even Pearl and Earl seemed to sense something was wrong. With quiet panic they scurried under the sofa. But Fannie never missed a beat, she had the biggest and brightest smile the girls had ever seen. In fact, her smile seemed to have stretched from one end of the room to the other.

"Okay," Fannie said, with her hands on her hips and in an authoritative yet festive voice. "Mrs. Crump is my seamstress and we have already picked out eight patterns we think would be appropriate for the girls to wear for my nuptials. They must in turn choose the pattern they like best for their own dress."

"Nuptials?" Tiffany whispered, frowning. Then, she went back to a grin. The wide-eyed girls wore silly grins on their lips in an air of excitement as they listened and watched their Aunt Fannie carefully stroking the fine fabrics.

"Girls! Girls!" Fannie said, clapping her hand twice in succession to get their undivided attention. "From the eight patterns I have selected, I want you to choose the pattern you like best for your gown. And I have the most mahvahlous idea ever. Guess what, my little angels?"

Nobody answered. There was an awkward, eerie silence in the room. They were all ears. Fannie beamed assuredly and said, "before long, each of you will seek your own rhythm in life. There is no better time to start this journey than at my wedding by wearing different gowns. Yes, the timing is just right for your individual styles to be discovered. I would love for each of you to pick the pattern that suits your individual personalities, styles, and shapes."

The silence in the room was deafening. Family members glanced around the room with wide leery eyes. With bated breath, they waited for the girls reactions. Even Pearl and Earl seemed to sense something was different, they scurried under the sofa, but Fannie had the biggest and brightest smile on her face the girls had ever seen. In fact, her smile seemed to have stretched from one end of the room to the other.

"What do you mean?" Brianna asked in disbelief. The silly expression on her face quickly turned into a disturbing frown.

Tiffany motioned a T sign with her hands and said, "Time out, Aunt Fannie. You mean you want us to wear different dresses?" She hoped she hadn't heard what she thought she had.

"Oh, no, we're gonna look weird, that's all, just plain weird" Silky said. And all our friends will be laughing at us," Tiffany said with her head cast down looking at Pearl. Brianna became increasingly agitated. Her bottom jaw relaxed, leaving her mouth hanging open. She felt awful about this bright idea not to mention on edge and disappointed and crampy too.

Freda and Mable were pleasantly surprised. Ruth, on the other hand, thought it was an excellent idea. "Oh, that would be just wonderful." She said, breaking the silence with a smile as bright as Fannie's.

Fannie was bubbling over with joy as she agreed with her sister-in-law, "No need for gloom and doom, you angels would look simply mahvahlous, and you would be setting a most unexpected new trend. How extraordinary would that be?" She was almost overwhelmed with her own idea. She paused, looked at Brianna, and said, "Sweetie, your mouth is opened." She continued, "Instead of looking like, umm . . . peas in a pod, each of your dresses would be a true expression of yourselves. You won't look weird, or whatever, that's simply ridiculous, it'll establish each of you girls as individuals . . . no more tired old replicas, let's put that to rest, it's boring." Fannie was beside herself with anticipation as she pushed her blonde hair out of her face and said, "You girls have different tastes, different likes and dislikes and different shapes. I want you to express your true selves at my wedding. It will be a truly liberating experience."

Noticing the puzzled looks on her nieces' faces, Fannie calmly said, "It'll work, girls. It'll work." The girls knew there was no point in arguing, it wouldn't matter anyway. It was clear their aunt's mind was made up.

The unspeakable was being spoken. The girls had never thought of being different, not even for a moment, especially for their Aunt Fannie's wedding, of all days.

Fannie realized that this would be a daunting task, but knew that it would ultimately be a learning experience for her favorite nieces, if she could only persuade them of how infinitely exciting it would be.

"Uh-uh . . . no way, we want to dress the same way for the wedding, Aunt Fannie. That's the way we want to look. That's the way it's supposed to be," Tiffany said, protesting with hands still on her hips.

"Yeah," agreed a frowning Brianna.

Fannie's calmness disappeared when she realized that the girls were not taking to her idea very kindly. At the same time, Freda was fanning with her tattered church fan hard and fast, realizing the girls hadn't bought into their Aunt Fannie's farfetched yet timely idea. She nervously fumbled with her locket and diamond tennis bracelet. Then, Freda tipped out back to sit on the porch swing. The friction inside was too much. Besides, she needed the fresh air. She was surprised to see it had stopped raining. Maybe we'll get some sun, she thought. Seconds later, Silky stormed out, barely holding back tears. When she saw her mother, she asked, "Ma, did you hear that?" She rushed over and hugged her mother without saying another word. Freda understood her daughter's feelings immediately.

"It'll work out fine, baby. You wait and see. It'll work out just fine," she said sympathetically. Freda stroked her daughter's hair. As a cool chill came into the air, Freda said, "Come on, sweetie. Let's go inside before we catch cold."

The women in the room quietly stayed out of the decision making. They thought that Fannie was being courageous; she did something that they only thought of.

"Well," said Fannie, "What do you girls want? Do you want to look like peas in a pod all your lives? This is going to be a mahvahlous way of expressing your true selves. Okay? Let's give it a try."

The seamstress stood over Tiffany's shoulders as she kneeled down on the multi-colored area rug that was strategically placed in front of the coffee table and began to pour over the eight patterns. Tiffany pondered for many minutes, trying to make the right choice. The women went back to eating.

"I think this one will look good on me," she said, looking squarely at her cousins.

It was an ankle length overlay dress with elbow length sheer sleeves and a matching cape. With the corner of her lips in the shape of an upside down U, Mrs. Crump said, "Are you sure, young lady?"

Tiffany responded with a small, "Yes."

Mrs. Crump quickly drew a circle around the pattern number 2308 and scribbled Tiffany's name next to it. She moved closer to Tiffany and took her measurements. Tiffany rubbed her nose when the seamstress came close to her.

The faint smell of old perfume on Mrs. Crump's paisley dress irritated her nose.

She quickly determined that the scent of her Aunt Fannie's tea rose perfume was of far better quality.

Meanwhile, Silky casually laid her eyes on an above the knee pattern with a matching sash that included a gathered waist tied in a big bow. The embroidered puff sleeves matched the embroidering around the scoop neckline. It reminded her of the elegant black dress her dad had bought her mother for an anniversary. She couldn't remember which one though, and at this point she didn't care.

Besides, she thought, the hem is short enough to show off her pretty legs.

"Are you sure, young lady? Is this the one you like most?"

"Yes, ma'am. I like the pretty sleeves," she said, but the hemline was what caught her eyes and that's what she really liked most.

"Goodness gracious. Wait a minute, Silky. Let me see which one you picked," Freda said after finishing her punch. She leaned over, adjusting her reading glasses. Freda glanced back at the pattern her daughter had chosen and said, "Silky, this is going to look darling on you. I just know it. You have shapely legs."

"Oh, yeah. That, too," Silky said, pretending she didn't pick that dress just to show off her legs. Silky smiled with more confidence now that her mother approved of her good taste, but she secretly wondered if her cousins felt sick like she did.

Mrs. Crump leaned over and circled pattern number 4509 and scribbled Silky's name next to it.

Taking the longest to decide, Brianna thought of the most sensible approach. Being the smallest of the three, she often suffered from having baggy stockings. She wanted something that would compliment her young figure and hide her thin legs at the same time. She studied the top four patterns. Then, she looked at the bottom four. Taking her time, she slowly said, "I think this one would look good on me."

Anxiously, Mable shoved the remainder of the sandwich in her mouth and grabbed a linen napkin to wipe her fingertips. She leaned over from the couch, fingered her small diamond studded earrings and said, "Honey, let me help you choose your dress. Now, let me see." She paused for a moment to look at the patterns and said, "I haven't done this in ages, girl. This is just too exciting. Don't you agree?" Her question went unanswered. "I know just what style would look sensational on you, sweetie."

"No, Momma," said an already agitated Brianna. "Let me do this myself. I'm big enough now to pick what I want to wear. I think the long straight dress with spaghetti straps and a split on the side would add inches to my height. Besides, a long dress would hide my stockings in case they sag. What do you think, Silky?"

"It's okay," Silky whispered softly.

"Yeah," Tiffany said, casting her eyes down.

Chapter Six Liberating Experience

"Okay, Mrs. Crump. This is the dress I want."

Mrs. Crump thought for a moment. Then, a little smile finally played around her lips for the first time that afternoon. She adjusted her reading glasses, lifting her nose slightly to see through the bifocal part of her glasses. She scribbled the pattern number 7112 down with Brianna's name next to it.

Mable gave Brianna's selection the once over and said, "Hmm, let me see, this is going to look fabulous on you, baby girl."

"I can't wait to see her in it," Fannie said. "Each one of you chose a different dress that compliments your extraordinary shapes and personalities."

The trio showed weary smiles and were only mildly amused at their Aunt Fannie's proud summation.

Mable proudly looked at her sisters and sister-in-law and said in a serious tone, "Fannie, you are absolutely right. They will always be cousins and hopefully best friends forever." Her eyes twinkled when she said, "My baby girl is gett'n so grown. You know I don't think Brianna would mind if I told you that she started her cycle yesterday." Mable smiled and boasted showing a flash of well kept teeth.

The experienced eyes of the women in the room were all aglow upon hearing the news. With curious grins on their lips, each head tilted to the side as their gasps turned into a chorus of "ahhhh's." Their jeweled fingers crossed over their bosoms as if it were a secret gesture, welcoming Brianna into womanhood.

"Momma, puh-leeze" begged the little girl in a tiny shaking voice. Her eyes still transfixed on the pattern, her body frozen with embarrassment.

Ignoring her daughter's wishes, Mable stubbornly continued, "Now, my baby wants to wear those ultra paper thin pads with wings. You know the kind you see on those television commercials? I tell you technology has invaded the sacred sanitary napkin. Would you have ever thought?" She rambled on, saying, "Whatever happened to the one and only Kotex? And check this out. They're archaic according to Brianna, archaic! Hump, girrrll, we had to race down to the drug store late last night before it closed to buy those *de-sign-er pads.*" Mable intentionally slowed down her verbalization that made matters worse. She dramatically put her hands on her full figure and swayed her body from one side to the other. "You know it's a shame they have so many different brands to choose from nowadays. Everything is new and improved, new and improved! I think it's pitiful not to mention confusing." The pitch of Mable's voice went up an octave higher as she engaged in her own cackle of laughter. She cleared her throat, and cocked her head to the side with her mouth unattractively gapped open. Her loud boastful laughter crammed the air along with the waving of her hands, creating her own ugly moment of excitement.

When the rude mockery of Brianna's womanhood was over, the damage was done, an eerie cloud of quietness descended among the room of women. They were quietly seated like spectators at a mud slinging contest, starring Mable, the only mud slinging bully.

The room became frigid, Mable sensed something was wrong. She glanced from side to side with wide eyes and tightly closed lips, noticing the disapproving looks in the eyes of everyone. She looked at her daughter and quickly covered her red lips with regret.

The window shook as the wind roared and fine rain crashed against the pane sounding more like chunks of icy hail.

The pain of embarrassment pierced deep into Brianna's little heart. To escape from being the side show of her mother's betrayal, she wanted to yell, "Just shut up, Momma! Please, shut up!", but she didn't. She remembered the word respect. Even though, her mother didn't respect her by not keeping her promise.

Brianna's stomach muscles throbbed in a rage of anger. She didn't know if the pain was from her mother's boastfulness or from the period cramps. She trembled as a silent flow of warm tears rolled swiftly from her eyes, crossing her perky little nose. There were so many tears that she couldn't wipe them all away. They just kept coming and coming. Tears of crushing humiliation stained the pattern book and fell onto the rug where the little girl kneeled, sobbing.

Chapter Seven

Something Evil

Diary,

I'm in the basement writing 'cause my daddy is yelling at the television. His team is losing, and he's burping really loud. I feel like writing a poem . . .

Weird Fannie, weird Fannie
She does things off the wall
Why can't she be ordinary?
All I ask is ordinary,
a little piece of ordinary
Would make my life complete!

There . . . That's the way I feel.

And I don't consider her our queen; she's just a regular aunt stealing our joy with a stupid idea.

I wanted to write about the "liberating experience" we had at our Aunt Fannie's house and how it made me feel. It was a disaster, the entire day was a disaster Diary, and it's all Aunt Fannie's fault for being weird. I really think she bumped her head or something and the way Aunt Mable went after Brianna, I was break'n out, I couldn't believe she could be that cruel to Brianna. She definitely needs a course in sensitivity. I even felt like giving her a piece of my mind too.

We should be able to pick the dress we want without our mother's interference.

I haven't heard from Tiffany or Brianna in three whole days after that. It seemed like forever to me. It's the longest time we have gone without speaking to each other since we were able to call each others' numbers without our mothers' help. That's not the half of it, Dairy. I got to let you know about this terrible feeling I had when we stopped speaking. The feeling was different from any other feeling I've ever had before. I'd much rather have detention or be grounded by my Momma. Those are only minor little tortures and they only take a day or two out of your life. After that, you're free to have fun again.

But without my cousin's friendship a weird feeling made my heart ache. It felt like something evil grabbed it out of my chest, stomped all over it and stuffed it back in. Then evil sat heavy on my chest, keeping the ache inside. Yeah . . . it feels just like that. My heart wasn't free, it was in pain.

I was good at pretending that it was okay though that we weren't speaking, but I thought of my cousins even more. We were like peas separated from the pod, we aren't supposed to be estranged. I didn't even feel like chewing sweet blueberry bubble gum. I didn't feel like eating dinner. My Momma even tried to give me a

sample of the blueberry pie she made. It looked good.
It was packed with more blueberries than her last pie,
but I didn't want that either. All I only wanted was for
me and my cousins to be best friends again.

I told my Momma how I felt, but I think she knew
all along. She said the best way to heal my heart was
to call my cousins and talk about my feelings. I asked
her how come they won't call me first. She said that it
takes a bigger person. It doesn't matter who calls first,
just as long as you girls talk.

Neva Schine lived alone in Sloan County's Mossy Creek
Valley ten miles outside of town. The population is a little over
a couple thousand well-to-do people. Neva owns all the land
as far as the eye could see. He like his place in the world
because he's well respected and liked.

It's normal for the rains to come down hard in Mossy
Creek. After the rain the sun would emerge and beautiful
blooming orchards and flowers of all species would show
their brilliant colors. The old valley became alive again as
the rain replenished the twisting waterway where the creek
flowed with ease, reestablishing familiarity. A new family of
frogs made their home on the edge of the creek hidden under
the yellowing honey locust trees and thick boxwood bushes.
Nervous deer ventured out of the fog towards the creek for
a hardy drink of cool water. Jack rabbits darted to and fro,
hopping their way from pine tree to huckleberry bush and
back into the woods again.

Chapter Seven Something Evil

Clean air and the soothing songs of birds was what Neva preferred in life, besides his Fannie that is. He was accustomed to a peaceful, easy lifestyle.

As a business man, Neva had owned the only haberdashery in Sloan County for thirty years. He built his three-bedroom ranch style house by reading architectural books and applying a lot of elbow grease. "It's through trial and error that you accomplish what you want," he always said. It was a quaint little house, nestled in the heart of the valley surrounded by lush mountains with just the right amount of vegetation.

His house is as pretty as a picture. In fact, it was featured in the *Pretty Homes* magazine after he completed it many years ago.

Neva's house is not a castle at all. It doesn't have a wrap around porch in which to hang a swing. It doesn't have a gazebo in which to confer or talk to spirits. The immaculate hard wood floors were free from rugs. And the uninviting front door with it's ordinary doorknob, made it a house of unimportance. But most of all, it doesn't have the excitement of a magic room. Neva is very different from fancy Fannie, he's laid back and ordinary.

Neva is a short, thin, copper colored man who wore cowboy boots and a cowboy hat that covered his balding head. He has a sprinkling of freckles on his nose. Under his nose, is a pencil lined mustache outlining his full lips. He is quite becoming, at least to Fannie, that is.

In spite of his small frame, he has a protruding stomach. He found delight in eating Fannie's collard greens, though. He loves Fannie's collard greens and learned how to cook them nice and tender, just like she does. He ate a plate of greens almost everyday and never complained about having too much. In fact, he had nine acres of land on the south side of his property cleared just for Fannie to grow her greens when she moves to the valley. Then she could feed Mossy Valley and Sloan County too.

Neva's passion wasn't designing and building houses. No, he's passionate about his antique automobile collection. So much so that he built a huge state of the art garage for his fleet of cars. His collection consist of three Lincoln Continentals, a 1978 Bentley, a 1958 Buick Roadmaster, 1957 Silver Cloud Rolls Royce, and a 1955 white Cadillac Coup de Ville, which was his favorite.

His best friend and best man, Eli Cunningham, is Neva's master mechanic. He keeps Neva's cars in mint condition. Eli owns and operates a small gas station in the Valley off Chestnut Boulevard. And like Neva, he is a bachelor, and has had his eye on Ruth for quite some time.

Underneath the Lincoln Continental, Eli laid on his back, fixing a small oil leak.

"Eli," yelled Neva, "Eli, can you hear me, good buddy?" He called again.

"Yeah, what's up?" Eli answered, without coming out from under the car.

"I'm going to pay my bride to be a visit. We're going to run some last minute errands before the wedding."

Eli slid from under the car with lightning speed with his wrench in his hand and the biggest toothy smile on his handsome dark face. He kept a dark due rag on his head whenever he was under a car just to keep the dirt out of his shiny black curly hair.

Eli eagerly asked, "You think you'll see Ruth there, huh?"

"I don't know. Fannie didn't say if Ruth was going to be there or not. If she's there, I'll put in a good word for you. See you later, buddy," Neva said with a smile as he decided to take the white Cadillac this time.

He revved the engine and slowly made his way through the muddy mountain trail onto the slick asphalt roads of the interstate.

Meanwhile, Fannie played with Pearl and Earl before Neva pulled up. The cats were making mad dashes through the house, jumping from sofas to chairs and onto tables and knocking over pictures of family and friends and knickknacks, too.

"What's wrong with you, crazy cats, why don't you take time out to purr a little bit? I have a notion to put you in the backyard, if you don't behave yourselves!" Fannie picked up the picture of little Justin Banks. Justin was her godchild. He lived overseas now with his military parents, Lillian and Richard.

"I haven't seen little Justin in about three years now. I guess he'll be a big old boy when I see him again. I wonder if they received my wedding invitation." She wondered out loud.

Out of the blue, Earl darted by while Pearl zigzagged through the pictures on the piano.

"Okay, okay, I'm going to feed you," Fannie said playfully.

She went into the kitchen cabinet and opened a can of cat food. She didn't have to call either of the cats. They ate as she spooned the moist gooey stuff into the dish.

"For goodness sakes, you guys act like I never feed you, you're just greedy. That's all. Just greedy cats," She affectionately scolded.

Fannie was prepared to leave as soon as Neva arrived. She had on her yellow rain slicker with the plaid zip out liner. The yellow plastic rain bonnet covered the top of her hair, leaving the yellow curls on her shoulders exposed to the elements. She carefully slipped her yellow galoshes over her shoes. They made a squishy sound, even though she hadn't worn them out in the rain yet. After that, she grabbed five bags of collard greens from the freezer and laid them aside in a brown paper shopping bag.

Fannie was concerned about many things now. She was slightly disturbed about the weather but very troubled about her nieces. Meditating was Fannie's way to connect to peace. That's what Fannie did after telephone conversations with her sisters confirmed that the girls hadn't spoken to each other after the fitting.

For the first time, Fannie realized that the girls might not have been ready to be their individual selves after all. She felt responsible, but deep down inside, she knew it was the right decision.

Everything seemed to have been closing in on Fannie, she stood still in the middle of the kitchen and closed her eyes to calm her nerves. Now she was in a place where the noisy thunder didn't faze her. She didn't worry if it rained or not on her wedding day, she didn't even care if her greens got too much rain. They were strong, enough to survive a monsoon. Fannie took advantage of this private moment to talk to Dear. She whispered, "Dear, what am I going to do about the girls? I love them so. You and Papa were always our Rock of Gibraltar, always saying things that needed to be said, when they needed to be said, always in the right way. What am I going to do? I don't have those same qualities. I pray that the girls will understand and get through this liberating experience as stronger individuals, loving and understanding each other more than before. I pray that they will forgive me too."

At that time, the vintage white Cadillac pulled into Fannie's cobblestone driveway next to the bike and stand. Neva lightly gripped the handrail as he walked up the five steps to the portico. He pressed the door bell once and waited for Fannie to open the fancy doors Fannie could see his short silhouette through the stained glass. Even that was handsome to her.

"Hump," Fannie said as she opened the door, "It stopped raining that fast," she said with her hands extended. Fannie leaned over and pecked Neva on the lips.

"Glad to see you, honey. How are you doing on this rainy day?" Fannie asked with her heavily made up face.

"I do fine, Fannie. I do just fine," he said slowly with his deep baritone voice. Fannie noticed that he was slowing down; he wasn't as spry as he used to be. Then he said, "Just can't wait to see my pretty bride in her wedding dress this Saturday. Then, I'll be better than fine!" He said, not really smiling but showing an even set of white teeth. Neva rarely used his lips to smile. His smile was in the twinkle in his eyes. Neva used to tell the girls that he smiled on the inside, from his heart, were it counts. Fannie remembered him saying that and calmly chuckled as she tucked her yellow locks further under her rain bonnet.

Neva's small frame barely covered the door way, "Are you ready, darlin'?"

"Yes, I'm ready, sweetie." She stepped outside of the house and then turned to lock the door.

Fannie felt the cool mist in the air and smelled the lingering rain.

"The girls haven't spoken since the fitting." Fannie blurted out, "they're miserable, Neva. What am I to do? I just got caught up in this mahvahlous idea about them being individuals and low and behold, the girls have stopped speaking to each other; I'm flabbergasted; I can't figure it out, Neva. I just can't figure it out," she said with deep furrows between her eyebrows joining her forehead. "Perhaps I was a bit too hasty. I don't feel at all peaceful today, my inners are all tied up in knots. I'm really very disappointed, now I've caused all this strife and nonsense with them not speaking and such. I'm supposed to be there for them, Neva!" She wringed her hands with a deepening worried look on her face.

Neva didn't like to see the worry lines of strife on his lovely bride's face. Whatever she wanted, he wanted to provide it for her or make it okay . . . just for his Fannie. It was important that Fannie was happy because, when she was happy, Neva was happy, too.

"Darlin', everything will work out for the best. You know my motto, just pray about it and leave it there. The girls don't know it now, but they'll know it soon enough. They're smart girls, you know. It'll work out. Watch and see. Yep, you watch and see Fannie. You know every time we're together, the sun is shining to me."

Fannie's worried face disappeared in an instant; she had stars in her eyes. She blushed like a schoolgirl smitten for the first time. She miraculously forgot about the damp, muddy, overcast day, but never forgotten about her troubled nieces. Fannie also remembered her prayer, and left it there, just like Neva said.

"Why, yes. I do believe I can see a little sunlight coming through those dark clouds other there, just like you said, see?" She said pointing as she gazed out at the sky.

While in truth, there wasn't a trace of sunlight, only low laying cumulus clouds ready to burst at the seams.

The rain only concerned Neva because it worried his Fannie. Otherwise, He accepted the rain for what it was; nourishment for the earth. It didn't bother him. He was a peaceful man, and the rain was peaceful, so it was all in natural order.

The first stop would be her antique shop. Fannie wanted to make sure that everything at the shop was okay. A bag of greens were for Hazel to take home.

The second stop would be Elmira's Flower Shop. Elmira was a friend of the family and a long time high school friend of Fannie's. She owned the only flower shop in Sloan County. Her specialty was exotic flowers.

Elmira was creating the flower arrangements for Fannie's wedding. Even though she didn't like collard greens, Fannie would give her an extra large bag and she said, "I want to make sure Elmira has the right color blue for the ribbons. "You know how crazy the girls are about their blue? Oh, and don't forget the church next door. Ms. Cora Lee is in charge of the sick and shut-in committee, so I know she can use a few bundles of these greens," she said with a smile. "After that, let's drive over to Sweeny's Sweet Confections." It was the largest bakery in town. Sweeny was the owner and head baker. He baked most of the wedding cakes in town. The rich buttery cakes were often stacked four and five tiers high and lavishly decorated with an array of flowers, leaves, and mounds of white fluffy icing. The bride and groom on the top were optional. Fannie chose to have leaves and flowers.

The family felt relieved, they teased Fannie reminding her that she wouldn't be able to decorate the cake with collard greenery because Sweeny was in charge of decorating the cake, his way, the proper way!

Fannie left Sweeny a big bag of collard greens, too.

Unlike Fannie, Neva wasn't as free spirited. Even eating in his immaculate cars was forbidden, but Fannie was comfortable with Neva's rules.

"Where to first, Poopsy?" He lovingly asked. "To the shop first and don't forget to stop at the church next door."

With a rare smile, he said, "I won't forget."

But Neva wasn't through reminiscing about the girls when they were babies. He said, "And Fannie don't you forget that I knew the girls before they were little bitty things. Yeah, that's right. I knew they were stars when each one of them was born. Remember when Silky took her first steps on that porch over yonder? She was something else, wasn't she, darlin'?"

"Yes, she was," Fannie said smiling as a rush of the past took over the moment.

"Remember when Silky used to push Tiffany's walker around with Tiffany in it? Lawd, that used to frustrate Tiffany to no end," Fannie said, laughing and coughing at the same time.

"It's a good thing Brianna was too young to be in a walker. I do believe both Silky and Tiffany would have pushed her around at the same time. Poor baby. and what about the time when I used to play "Ring Around the Roses" with Silky. She could barely walk, trying to keep up with me with her strong legs and pudgy little feet. Neva, do you remember that?" She asked with a bright smile.

With a twinkle in his eye, Neva graciously nodded his head. His deep baritone voice rolled out a slow "Yeahhh," through his mocha colored lips. It was almost in slow motion. Fannie continued, "And when it was time to say 'we all fall down,' Lawd, that girl would flop down so hard on her precious little bottom, and didn't feel a thing either. God bless her little heart. You know, those pampers were good and padded! Lawd knows, if I had flopped down like that, I'd be right there still on that porch waiting for you to come help me up."

Neva nodded his head and slowly rolled out another deep, "Yeahhh," with the same twinkle in his eyes.

"And remember the tea parties, Neva? The ones they had in the gazebo with their faces all made up and such, holding tight to their brown baby dolls you gave them for Christmas?"

Again Neva nodded and slowly rolled out another, "Yeahhh," this time with a warm smile you can see.

"Those were the good old days . . . priceless days, absolutely priceless," she said with a far away look in her eyes.

She began softly singing the familiar nursery rhyme, the one she had sung to her three favorite nieces many, many times when they were toddlers . . . .

"♫Ring around the roses, pocket full of posies, ashes, ashes, we all fall down . . ♫"

As her voice faded, she paused and took a deep breath. She looked down wistfully into her fiancé's round face studying his eyes. Neva was just as moved as Fannie. They looked into each other's dreamy eyes and held hands. There was an incredibly solid bond between the two. Sharing the ups and downs of the past bonded them in magnificent love.

Chapter Eight

Forbidden Zone

Diary,

I'm sitting in my bedroom closet 'cause it's the warmest place in the house. Guess what I have on? I have on a bra, an old undershirt, a sweatshirt, my school cardigan buttoned all the way up and my fleece lined jacket! My Momma has lost her mind with this "change of life" thing. I wish she'd hurry up and change. I'm freezing!

Okay Diary, this is how it happened, it's not complicated at all, I just decided to be the bigger person like my momma said. It wasn't easy though, . . . when I called them, I couldn't think of one thing to say. I felt real stupid. I wished that I had magical powers to help me. I know one thing though, it's easier to laugh and be silly than to say what's really on your heart . . . for real. It was the first time, Diary, I had trouble expressing myself to my cousins—my used to be best friends. All I know is, if they told me they wanted to be best friends again, I'd say "Thank you, Lawd," and I'd promise to love them for the rest of my life . . .

and their lives, too! I'm going to tell you everything, Diary, everything, everything, everything—especially about how we became best friends again.

Well, first of all, I waited 'til my Momma went to Spiegel's Supermarket & Deli to get a quart of soy milk and a loaf of sourdough bread (YUCK!). She was cranky that day anyway; I was hoping she'd be in a better mood when she returned.

Daddy was in the den, laying on his recliner under tons of blankets with his wool argyle socks on. I bought those for him last Christmas, so he was all comfy listening to the television while he rested his eyes. Everything was perfect. I tiptoed through the main hallway where a portrait of Dear and Grandpa Busby hung. Next to the picture was the thermostat, better known as the "forbidden zone." I put one hand over my grandparent's eyes as I studied the thermostat for a minute. I knew they couldn't see I just felt comfort in hiding some things that I shouldn't do. Especially my momma's thermostat policy.

Well she had it on 62°, so I bumped it up just a little to 98°. I wasn't worried about my daddy. He wouldn't even feel the difference.

Anyway, I think better when I'm not cold. Besides, I also promised myself I wouldn't forget to turn it back down before my Momma got home.

I dialed Tiffany's number first. Aunt Ruth answered. I said, "Hi, Aunt Ruth, can I speak to Tiffany?" Aunt Ruth asked about my Momma and my daddy before she called Tiffany to the phone.

Tiffany said, "Hello."

I said, "Hi." There was silence on the line.

Then, I said, "How come you didn't call me?"

Then, she said, "I thought you were mad at me."

Then, I said, "No, girl. I'm not mad at anyone."

Then, there was silence again. I started to sweat. I unbuttoned my jacket and took it off.

I waited for the magic powers to kick in, but they never did.

Then I said, "Let's get Brianna on the line, too."

Soon, all three of us were on the same line. Brianna spoke timidly when she said she thought we were mad at her for having skinny legs. She said, "Aunt Fannie told us to pick the dress that would fit our shapes and personalities. And that's what I did. I'm sorry that I have skinny legs. If I could change them, I would, but I can't!" Then, she started to cry.

Then, Tiffany said, "I thought you were mad at me 'cause I'm big boned."

I didn't say a word. Besides, there was nothing to be mad at me about—I'm just about perfect.

I still felt sad, though. I could tell Tiffany felt sad, too.

I said. "I'm just saying—this is real stupid, I'm not mad at anyone."

"Me, either," Tiffany said.

Then, Tiffany started to make sense when she said, "This is going to be Queen Fannie's special day. We can at least dress differently for just one day and be happy about it. We can always go back to dressing the way we like, you know, like peas in a pod!"

I said, "Yeah, one day won't hurt."

Brianna stopped sniffling and said, "Well, does this mean we're best friends again?"

I know Tiffany had a smile on her face when she said, "Yeah." I heard it in her voice.

I said, "Hallelujah! Thank you, Lawd. My heart is free. I have my cousins and we're best friends again!"

Then, the next thing I heard was the garage door open and close. Then I heard my momma's blood curdling scream, you know, like she was in the movies or something, it freaked me out. I've never heard such ugly noise coming from my momma's pretty lips.

I slammed the phone down so fast that I forgot to tell my cousins bye.

Scared to death, I made a mad dash past the den and peeked in. Daddy wasn't there. I saw a big puddle of sweat on his leather recliner, inside of the puddle was his trousers, one of his argyle socks I bought him for Christmas, his sweater and one of his blankets. "Dang, what happened to my daddy? Did he evaporate like the wicked witch? Oh no . . . that can't be. I killed my daddy," I cried. That was all I could think of. Then suddenly I lost myself in the imaginary world and it became clear, so very clear. Without a doubt my picture was plastered on the Sloan County Tabloid, the large lettering above it read, "Pint Sized Murderess Accused of Patricide". Of course, Cool Aid was there to protect me from the rude, elbowing paparazzi and their

Chapter Eight Forbidden Zone

blinding cameras. He held me close to his masculine chest as I buried my face there from the press. I cried, "This isn't true. I love my daddy. I love my daddy very much. This is all an awful mistake. This can't be happening to me. I haven't even started my period yet, I couldn't have done this." I cried uncontrollably. Suddenly, I snapped back to reality when I heard momma scream my name out loud, for the third time. When I got to the kitchen, I saw my parents standing beside the kitchen table half dressed, frustrated and angry. My daddy was in his shorts with one sock half way off his foot and the other one missing. His under shirt was drenched in sweat and a large embarrassing drop hung from his nose. He was frantically fumbling, trying to cover momma with his other blanket. At one glance I noticed momma's carefully pressed hair was now a full blown afro. From the corner of my eye, I saw the trail of momma's clothes, leading from the garage onto the kitchen floor! Well needless to say I was sweat'n bullets myself because I had no defense for my silly action, I just wanted to talk to my cousins, that's all. I knew I was in trouble, big time! That's the real deal and the reason why I'm in this dusty closet writing in you.

The rain let up some, and the bright sun made an effort again to shine through the remaining patchwork of low clouds.

It was a damp, muggy day, and it was only days before the wedding.

"Lawd, what on earth am I going to do? I pray that the sun comes out nice and strong and dries the property around the house with its warm rays," Fannie said, speaking to the spirits of the house. Fannie turned around and put on her glass teakettle to brew her tea.

She looked around the organized clutter. To her, her house was full of treasures. There was a multitude of small multi-colored area rugs, everywhere. Long thick draperies hid the daylight, and silk flowers and eyelet doilies and other doodads occupied every vacant spot of the tables. She couldn't take accurate inventory even if she tried. All the stuff she had collected from her travels over the many years made her house looked cluttered like the shop, in a small way of course. The formal portraits of her mother and father hung over the mantel. The rest of the family and friends' portraits hung from walls or adorned the tables all over the house. They were a part of who she was. They were a constant reminder of past lives. She didn't know how she was going to tell her family that Neva was going to retire and sell his haberdashery and build their dream home in the Valley. This was a difficult secret for Fannie to keep.

The teakettle whistled. She passed the long hall mirror and stopped to take inventory of herself. "Gosh, it doesn't look as though I've lost a pound. Oh, it's probably this bulky blue robe and these big fury slippers. They make me appear bigger than I really am." Fannie didn't like the slippers too much. They were a Christmas gift from Tiffany, but Earl loved them, turning him into a nuisance as he ran behind her every step and chased after the tails that dragged behind the furry footwear.

Fannie strolled into the kitchen and poured herself a cup of Chinese green tea into a white porcelain teacup with the matching saucer trimmed in gold. They were from a fine china set of eight that Dear received as a gift on her wedding day many, many years ago. Fannie carefully took a warm tea biscuit from the oven and smeared the top with a dollop of her homemade blueberry jam and decided to incorporate her snack with a small plate of greens. She settled down at her metal kitchen table. As always she blessed her food and extended her delicately painted right pinky in the air as she enjoyed her tea. Fannie flipped her golden locks away from her eyes and carefully lifted the cup and poured the overflow from the matching saucer back into the cup and sipped some more.

Relaxed, she relished the quiet moment with meditation and peaceful talk to Dear and Pa.

Chapter Nine

A Claim of Fame

Diary,

I really didn't kill my daddy that day, but my momma had a fit about the thermostat. She said some angry words, telling me that as long as I lived under her roof, I was never to touch that thermostat again. Then, real mean like, she said, "Do you understand, young lady?" She wasn't playing. Her face was all frowned up. She pointed a mean looking finger in my face. That's when I saw the dark side of my momma, and it scared me. It scared me a lot!

That's why I'm writing from underneath my bed covers again. She grounded me for two days. Now, it's time for medical attention. You know what she said? She said she felt like ice skating naked. Diary, you believe that? She needs to chill-out; it's not all that serious. Where is she going to find an ice skating rink here in Sloan County?

Well anyway, did I tell you about the time Fruity the stray dog managed to dig a hole under the fence and get into my Queen Fannie's vegetable garden?

Fruity used to belong to Cecil Cartwright, that's the kid who lives three blocks away. Cecil goes to school in Boone County but we're in the same grade.

See, Fruity is an adorable look'n dog; you know the kind you see on commercials.

Anyway, queen Fannie was watering and whispering sweet nothings to the small herb garden she had in the kitchen window. When that adorable pest clawed his way under the fence, making a deep dark hole into the vegetable garden.

I saw him, I witnessed everything. He ran pass the okra and the field peas with his hungry eyes dead fixed on the Queens bouquet of collards. He sniffed the greens for a quick second before he started munching on her most prized vegetable, and oh my goodness, all heck broke loose. (I'm not allowed to say the other word.) Queen Fannie was fuming. Her eyes popped out. Her mouth was opened just wide enough to see her top and bottom teeth glued together. Well, they looked like they were glued together to me. Her bracelets rattled as she grabbed the old worn out broom from the broom closet. I thought she had grown wings for real. Just like me running down those seventeen stairs from the magic room, remember?

Well, the mad queen just about flew into the yard with that old broom swinging high in the air and her blue furry slippers slipping on and off her feet. The tails on her slippers were flying and the weird flip-flop sound of the slippers slapped the sole of Queen Fannie's bare feet. She was trying to keep them on while running, making large strides into the yard down to where that crazy dog stood chewing on her bouquet of collards. Diary, I thought I felt the ground shake.

Earl, with his dumb self, decided to merrily chase after Queen Fannie's furry tails as she ran toward Fruity. It was kind of funny though. See . . . it happened so fast, all we saw was the back of our Queen Fannie waving that broom in the air, yelling, "I'm gonna get that dog-gone dog, I'm gonna wring his neck, then I'm gonna hit him up side his noggin with this here broom." Her long blonde curls were flying, and her oversized bottom jumped up and down, up and down, just like a washing machine. It was something else. I told myself it wasn't funny, but I held my hand over my mouth so the laugh wouldn't come poppin' out like it did when Camischa insulted Ms. Thunder that day in school. Only this was funnier, but I have learned how to control myself. I decided that I'd have to pray for that ugly dog . . . for real! After Queen Fannie scared the mess out of Fruity, he ran back to that black hole under the fence with his tail between his legs. He didn't growl or nothin'. He just scrambled back through the darkness to the safe side of the fence in the nick of time. He was about to get clobbered big time.

Queen Fannie was out of breath and sweating. She dropped the broom near the red peppers. She picked up Earl and carried him back to the porch. She sat on the porch swing and began to swing. Sweat formed on top of her lip like an invisible mustache while streams rolled down from underneath her wig onto her cheeks.

Breathing fast and heavy, Queen Fannie properly said, "It's utterly hot out here." Then, she asked for one of us to get her a Diet Coke. "And, baby, make sure there's plenty of ice in the glass, hear?" Tiffany jumped for the privilege and ran to the kitchen and returned with a frosty glass of coke packed with ice. Queen Fannie sat for a long while pettin' Earl, lookin' hard at that black hole under the fence and sucking on a ice cube. That was funny, Diary. We wanted to bust out laughin', but we didn't 'cause we knew how Queen Fannie felt about her bouquet of collards. ♥

"Practice makes perfect. Practice makes perfect," Mrs. Crump sung in a high-pitched tone as she pounded a crude rendition of the wedding march on the family piano. Fannie eagerly watched from her overstuffed armed chair with her feet comfortably resting on the leopard-covered footstool as her nieces rehearsed their wedding march in the living room. Her mind wasn't on the rehearsal so much as it was on the locket she borrowed from Freda. Oh how she wished her parents could be here for her wedding.

Little Brianna would be the first to march. She carried her cheer leading pom poms in place of the boutique. Tiffany, who would be second, carried her microphone from her karaoke recorder. Silky simply carried the picture of Cool Aid, the one she took when he won the oratory contest in school the first time. All three cousins were dressed in identical t-shirts and denim overalls.

"No, no, no, girls, you must step to the rhythm of the beat, with finesse, like this," Mrs. Crump instructed.

"Now, look at my feet," she said as she quickly took two giant steps to get from behind the piano and onto the area rug next to the girls.

"Now, watch me." She threw her shoulders back and her bosom appeared astronomically larger. She gazed up at the ceiling. She held her head high. Her arms were held out and away from her hips, while her hands gracefully played in the air. She said, "Now, watch me carefully." She daintily took baby steps in her big clumpy comfort shoes, humming the bridal tune . . .

"♫ Dum . . . dum . . . dee . . . . dum ♫."

The girls were beside themselves as they held back the explosion of laughter that had been building up in the pit of their stomachs ever since they had met her. Brianna flashed a glance to Silky, and Silky knew that Brianna was looking for permission to rudely bust out laughing, so she pursed her lips in such a way as to hold it in, but she couldn't hide the tell tale expression of silliness on her face.

Tiffany, on the other hand, didn't hesitate and had abandoned the idea of being polite. She let out an explosion of laughter loud enough to drown out both of her cousins.

"Come on, girls. Behave," sung Mrs. Crump. "And put some oomph into your steps."

"Now, let's see how mature we can be. Follow me. This is not a funeral. It's a wedding, girls. A very fine, spectacular wedding fit for royalty, a sight to behold, yes . . . a sight to behold." Her eyes mesmerized looking high at the ceiling with

Chapter Nine A Claim of Fame

her hands clutched tightly together in great expectation. She continued to take baby steps, keeping her nose high in the air.

"Yeah, Silky, show how mature you are," smirked Tiffany.

"Oh, look whose talking, Miss Goody two shoes," said Silky sucking her teeth.

"Yeah, but you're the one who started laughing first," smirked Brianna, pointing to Tiffany.

"Well," Tiffany said, taking the rubber band out of her pony tail and brushing back the loose ends with her hands and putting the rubber band back on again, "Y'all can play around if you want, but this is the first fifteen minutes of a long life of stardom for me. *I AM* going to be a star you know? I'm gonna have lots of money, mansions, designer clothes and an entourage of wanna be's!" Then Tiffany closely imitated Mrs. Crump, making tiny baby steps on the rug.

"Well, at least, I have Cool Aid. He's the light of my life. The sugar in my gum, he's what makes my heart skip a beat. I Looove Cool Aid." Silky said with her hands on her hips.

Both Tiffany and Silky turned and looked at Brianna.

"Well, what's your claim to fame?" Tiffany asked with a devious grin. "Yeah," Silky said, "What's your claim to fame?" Little Brianna's brown eyes darted around; searching for something that she believed would make her important like her cousins. Her pretty face lit up like a light. Excited, she naively blurted out with a smug smile, "At least, I got my period first!"

A frizzled Mrs. Crump rolled her eyes up to the ceiling and sighed, "Oh Lawd, what nonsense."

Chapter Ten

Sweet Spirit

Diary,

First of all, I didn't write anything about what happened the other day at the castle. I wasn't a happy camper when I left, none of us were. It was the worst meeting ever. Because of those hurtful words Aunt Mable said about Brianna and her period and all. She needs a crash course in sensitivity. And second of all, we won't be wearing the same style bride maid dresses, you know we're into the pod thing!

But I'm happy about Ms. Thunder moving my desk to the other side of the room away from Camisha Tolbertson. I'm glad, because I really don't want to act the fool like I did before, laughing and everything, making Ms. Thunder feel uncomfortable about her big butt. Besides, it relieves me from the drama and foolishness that goes on in class.

What happened last week Diary isn't foolishness though, it's the real deal. And because secrets are for telling; I decided this secret will be between you, me and Cool aid. It's top secret. It's such a big secret that

I'm going to fold this page in half, you know, hot dog style. Ms. Thunder taught us that if a page is folded over, no one is supposed to open it. Hot dog style sounds too babyish though, so I'll call it vertical, the proper way. Well anyway it's like respecting the secret, so it'll stay a secret. I didn't even tell my cousins when we were at the headquarters last week.

So I'm going to tell you everything, everything, everything. Right down to the juicy details, okay?

Well anyway . . . last Wednesday, me and Cool Aid decided to sneak off the lunch line and ren-dez-vous to the gym. I got there first then came my prince charming with his hair freshly braided. He was sooo cute. Well anyway, the door under the bleachers was open. We peeped inside. It was nice and dark under there. We knew it would be the perfect place to be alone. With my hand holding tightly in his, he lead me inside the underworld of the bleachers and I closed the creaking door behind us. We were in complete smelly darkness, alone for the first time. We didn't say anything to each other when my soul mate began kissing me on my cheek and then on my neck, then he nibbled at my ear. I was excited and began squeezing his sweaty hand harder. He was taking too long though, kissing me on the cheek and then down to my neck and then up to my cheek again, up and down, up and down, so when his moist lips came up to my cheek for the forth time, I turned my head kind'f fast so that our lips would touch. And WOW, it was complete wonderfulness, his lips felt like sweet, fluffy marshmallow against mine.

My heart pounded in a different way, I thought it would leap out of my chest with happiness . . . for real. The light in my heart became a beacon for love. It was a feeling I have never felt before. Well I thought it was a light from my heart, but it was the light from the gym that I saw. We didn't hear the door creek open but there in the doorway stood a hobbit sized person with one hand on a large hip and the other flashed a bright flash light in our faces. It was Ms. Thunder, aka, Ms. Thunderbutt. Diary, that ren-dez-vous got me and Cool Aid sent to the principal's office, while Ms. Thunder called our parents. I heard her. I heard her telling my Momma where she found us and what she thought she saw.

Well, momma took time off her job to sign me out of school early that day. She didn't say a word to me all day long. I stayed in my room away from her glaring eyes. I didn't want to annoy her or anything and I didn't know what to expect. I was scared. I held on to Cool Aid's picture and thought of what a wonderful boy he was. ♥

Momma waited for daddy to come home from work that evening and that's when I was lectured by both of my parents. Momma was extra mean, and became so emotional that she slapped her church hat on her head and dragged me down to Greater Light Baptist Church so that Reverend Katrill could pray over me. We sat in a secluded area of the sanctuary where the light was dim and the air was kind'f cool. That's where Reverend Katrill began to pray. He placed his heavy hand on my freshly braided extensions and prayed that the Lawd would deliver me from the sinful grip of for-ni-cation. All the while momma sat there wiping her teary eyes with a paper towel and fanning her face at the same time. I was irritated Diary and really scared because I wasn't sure what that word for-ni-cation meant, it didn't sound very nice. I thought Reverend Katrill was trying to pray that feeling of true love out of me. He kept repeating, "deliver the evil lore of lust from your precious child, Lawd." But I didn't feel evil, and it wasn't lust, it was love . . . I felt true love. I didn't want Reverend Katrill go praying the love out of me. He made a little happiness and a little kiss out of something dirty. I started thinking about Cool Aid more and more, I truly believe I love him.

I felt cornered by momma and Reverend Katrill. Anyway he was taking too long praying over me and he was definitely too loud so I decided to be defiant. I closed my eyes real tight and prayed asking God to make him shut up. When that didn't help I put my fingers in both ears and started humming under my breath, "Jesus Loves Me, Yes I Know." All the while I remembered seeing the sparks in my daddy's eyes fade when momma told him why she signed me out of school early. The look that daddy gave me still haunts me and when he said "where . . . under the bleachers?" In an unusually high pitch tone, you can tell that he was struggling to remain clam, but sternly said, "what in the world?, not my little girl." He was so disappointed and that really made me cry. I was ashamed for kissing cool aid but not sorry for feeling that awesome feeling of love.

"Take out the fortune teller; Brianna, let's see who's going to tell old man Duffy off," said Silky as the nearly empty bus turned the corner headed toward Harmony Grove Nursing Home.

Tiffany complained, "Let me tell him off once and for all. How would you like to be called Vanilla? I do have color to my skin, you know," she said pointing to the faded tan on her white arms. "Anyway, vanilla is boring," she said sulking and folding her arms.

Both Brianna and Silky looked at each other with sad smiles.

"Well now, brown sugar is the name that describes me best, if he called me that, it would be a different story." said Silky.

"But chocolate chip," she said in an indignant high pitch tone, "do I look like a chocolate *CHIP* to you? Besides you know a measly *CHIP* is a weak morsel of a whole. Just look at me cousins", she said as she searched in her denim purse for the picture Tiffany took of her last week in the magic room. Look at me, she pointed to her highly made up self, wearing one of her aunts wigs.

"I may not be perfect but I am whole. Thank you very much."

Silky, kissed her picture and placed it back in her purse. She took out a pack of blueberry bubble gum and pealed off the wrapper and stuffed it into her mouth.

She wiggled her backside attempting to gain more space in the double seat that occupied the three of them.

"Is that blueberry bubble gum? I love blueberry bubble gum. It's good and sweet," said Tiffany.

She quickly took a stick of gum without asking; so did Brianna.

"Now how are we going to tell him off?" Tiffany asked with excitement.

"That's easy, let's jack him up first, then tell him off, and um, we'll respect him later." Silky said as an after thought.

She chewed her gum slowly with a conniving smile.

"Ah, let's be serious, pleaded Brianna. Momma said we've got to be diplomatic about this, we're young ladies you know." She said rolling her eyes.

"Who said I wasn't serious," Snickered Silky.

"Hmmm, this gum hits the spot," said Tiffany, satisfying her sweet tooth.

The girls ignored the sound of the noisy windshield wipers that made the way clear for the bus driver to stop at the curb. Two older men boarded the bus. One was a bearded man, the other was a blind man who held on tightly to his guide dog's leash. They both sat in the front row on the other side of the girls.

They spoke quietly to each other with a laugh or two. Then they were quiet.

The girls animatedly carried on their conversation about Mr. Duffy.

"He probably was a mean man when he was young. That's why his family never visits him. He never has any company-not even on important holidays like Christmas." Said Tiffany,

"Yeah, he's a crabby old man. That's why he has hair growing out of his ears," said Brianna chewing wildly and talking at the same time. She took out the folded fortuneteller.

It was made from glossy white paper that was decorated with a watermark pattern of daisy's all around. It was folded all nice and neat. Neat, just like Brianna.

"You know old man Duffy makes me so mad when he calls me olive oil. Besides, I'm a young lady now, and Brianna is my name." She said with a scowl of conviction on her face.

Brianna took out her blueberry of Paradise lip-gloss rolling the greasy stuff over her petite lips and rolling her eyes at the same time. She wiggled trying not to get squished against the inside of the bus and Silky.

"What ever," Silky said unmoved.

"Where's the brown lip liner. I need to outline my lips, like Aunt Fannie does." She said.

"We don't need to outline our lips." said Brianna frowning, that's Aunt Fannie's way, it doesn't have to be ours too," she said finally making sense . . .

Tiffany just listened while looking out at the rain.

"Hump," Silky said, and took out her lip liner and lightly outlined her lips. Then she smeared Brianna's lip-gloss generously on her full lips. She pressed her greasy lips together to smudge the dark line blending it into the blueberry color.

The bus shifted to the side as it came to a red signal light and stopped.

Tiffany looked at Silky and noticed how ridiculous her already full lips appeared, she handed her a tissue from her purse, and said, "Here Silky, you need to dab a little of the gloss off your lips, it makes your lips look bigger and darker than they really are," She said.

"No it doesn't" snapped Silky,

"Besides, I was born with these pretty lips; I just want to accentuate them." She stubbornly said, and then she pressed her lips together again to give them an equal smearing of gloss.

By this time, Brianna had her thumbs and her index fingers in the folded areas of the paper fortune teller moving them quickly several times back and forth unfolding and folding it again and again then she stopped.

"Okay now, pick a number," she said.

Tiffany said, nonchalantly, "Two."

"Okay," said Brianna, and started quickly moving her fingers again, back and forth, and back and forth and stopped.

"Okay" said Brianna, "now pick a color."

There were four in which to choose from, yellow, blue, pink and purple.

"I always pick blue, but this time I'll give everybody a break and pick, uh . . . purple this time," said Tiffany.

"Halleluiah," said Silky relieved then blew a large blue bubble.

Brianna opened the folds of the fortuneteller to reveal Tiffany's fortune.

It said, *"You will be rich."*

Tiffany smiled, and said "but I already know that." Then blew a small blue bubble.

"Okay, Brianna it's your turn."

"Give me the fortune teller," said Silky.

"Okay." Smiled Brianna as she eagerly watched Silky move her fingers back and forth, then back and forth again before stopping.

"Pick a number," said Silky.

Brianna thought for a minute and said "uh, Seven."

Then Silky repeated moving her fingers back and forth several times.

"Okay," now pick a color."

Brianna waited for Silky to a stop before choosing the color blue.

Silky opened the folds and read her fortune. She read, *"God loves you."*

Brianna eyes shined brightly as she said, "I know that too."

"Okay now give it to me so I can tell your fortune," said Tiffany.

"Okay," said Silky, but we got to get off the next stop so hurry."

"Okay, Okay," said Tiffany moving her fingers fast.

"Pick a number," she said.

Without much thought Silky said, "four."

Then Tiffany's fingers moved like a streak of lightning four times when she saw the nursing home coming into view.

Silky noticed a van from Miss Elmira's Exotic Flower Shop was parked in the front of the nursing home delivering flowers.

"Pick a color fast Silky, hurry up."

Tiffany said chewing as fast as her fingers moved.

"Pink," said Silky as she stood up.

Tiffany opened the fold in haste and read Silky's fortune, it read,

"You are brave."

"See . . . that does it Silky you're the lucky one who gets the chance to tell old Mr. Duffy off."

Tiffany said with a weary grin.

The girls stood up waiting patiently for the two elderly men and the dog to exit first. The man who wasn't blind had watery eyes as he gave the girls a warm smile. He helped his friend make his way off the bus. The girls ignored them and continued to plot their strategy.

"Yep, the fortune teller never lies." Said Brianna with her hands stretched out waiting for Tiffany to smear the small tube of lip-gloss on her lips too.

"Okay," said Brianna, "But Momma told me that we can't be rude you know; we have to respect our elders. Okay?"

"Okay, Brianna, I won't be rude", said Tiffany.

Brianna glanced at Tiffany and nodded in agreement.

"Okay?" Brianna said," looking firmly at Silky in a no nonsense tone.

Silky didn't reply.

"Like I said, we didn't get permission to tell him off, we've got to be respectful", she repeated a little louder and in a more forceful than before.

"Momma said . . ."

Before Brianna could finish her sentence, Silky casually raised the palm of her hand in Brianna's face halting the rest of the stupid rules and angrily blurted out, "Bunk that Brianna, it's playback time," showing her disapproval by moving her head from side to side.

"No offence to Aunt Mable but, remember what I told you what Mr. Duffy did to me?"

Both cousins said "oh yeah," in a secretive whisper while gawking at Silky.

But Brianna really hadn't forgotten, though.

"Stop look'n at me like I did something wrong, remember I told you about it right after it happened. And it's true; when I was handing Mr. Duffy his blanket he grabbed it from me and slyly touched my boobs." She said, convinced she had been violated.

Briana and Tiffany covered their lips with their fingers in disgust, there was an awkward moment of silence between the three girls. But Tiffany felt a tickling sensation of laughter wedged in her throat then a smile begin to play around the ends of her lips and without hesitation, she burst out in uncontrollable laughter and said, "but . . . but how can you tell if someone's feeling your boobs, when your padded bra is stuffed to the gills with toilet paper; she said laughing and pointing at Silky's chest. Silky felt betrayed by the wild laughter it stabbed at her feelings and disrespected the sisterhood. What made matters worst, Brianna joined in on the laughter, validating Tiffany's accusation by saying "yeah," pointing at Silky's chest while still giggling she added, "I saw two balls of toilet paper in your purse Silky when I borrowed a pencil for math class the other day."

Silky felt betrayed and the butt of a cruel joke. It was painful to see her cousins enjoying her misfortune with total disregard to their bond and her feelings.

"I don't have to lie, I don't have to lie said a teary Silky, in an elevated whisper."

She noticed the bus driver peering at them through the rear view mirror, then stopped at a red light again.

Silky continued, "Besides" she whispered wiping away tears, I'm a victim of an old mans touch and this isn't a laughing matter this is serious, very serious.

Silky lowered her shaken voice even more and said, "He even put his hand on my knee one day. He made me feel" . . . she stopped to search for the right word and said . . ."well, uncomfortable, and I'm still furious. And you shouldn't be laughing at me, 'cause it's the truth." Her voice became stronger when the laughter stopped, and a more serious expression was etched on her cousin's faces.

"I think he's one of those predators, you know those nasty men who prey on kids." Silky finally said pouting with folded arms.

"Oh you mean a pedi—um—no I think you pronounce it ped-o-phile," interjected Brianna, the most informed reader of the trio. "Yeah, that's the right word—pedophile", she concluded with certainty. I know what you're talking about Silky, I read about those weirdoes in a book and I remember a nasty web site popped up on my monitor one day discussing their twisted behavior, ugh!"

"Ewww, that's just plain nasty." Tiffany chimed in with her lips curled up in disgust. She shook her head from side to side, her body stiffened with the very thought of it.

"Yeah", now you see I wasn't making it up," Silky said her eyes deliberately squinting and jaws tight. She unfolded her arms and made both hands into fist, just like she was preparing for battle. You didn't tell anybody did you?" Silky's words sounded more like a threat, than a question.

"No Silky, I swear I didn't tell a soul", said Tiffany, "me either," Brianna timidly confessed. However, Brianna became agitated and felt compelled to tell the whole truth and said "well . . . I almost told momma the other day when we were talking about Mr. Duffy, but I didn't, I didn't tell, I cross my heart and hope to die, Silky. I didn't say a word about what that ugly old man did to you." confessed Brianna.

After regaining control, Silky said,

"So now you see", she said with one hand on her hip, shifting her shoulders back giving herself a more demanding posture. She was more convinced that Mr. Duffy was guilty of being a dirty old man . . . then she calmly ended her admission with a sigh of relief and said . . ."so that settles that, he's a pedophile person and he needs to be dealt with . . . case closed."

But do we still have to be respectful, like momma said?" Brianna asked nervously. You know what she said?

Silky glared at Brianna and said . . .""bunk that" just spare me the boring details Brie, I got this."

Brianna and Tiffany were wide eyed, and uneasy by Silky's sassy, no nonsense attitude.

And even though the details for the battle with Mr. Duffy were unclear and muddled at best, it was set for execution anyway.

The bent over, fist swinging, high stepping trio were on a mission. They only slowed down briefly for the deliveryman who was blocking their way, he was carrying a beautiful spray of red carnations doted with baby's breath.

"I wonder who they're for" said Tiffany, pointing to the beautiful flowers, while glancing around looking for Mr. Duffy.

"Who knows?" Shrugged Silky.

Upon entering the reception area the girls were greeted by Mrs. Agnes Johnson behind the reception desk.

"Hi girls," she said in a high pitched, pleasant voice. "We haven't seen hide nor hair of you girls in over a week."

She was always thrilled to see the girls.

"Good to see you on this rainy day, y'all look so pretty in blue."

"Hi Mrs. Johnson," the girls said with endless smiles.

"Look here," said Mrs. Johnson, "I'm so glad to see you girls back speaking again." She said wide eyed, with an inquisitive voice.

The girls looked at each other in amazement.

In an apologetic manner, Mrs. Johnson lightly covered her mouth with her arthritic fingers, and confessed.

"I know it's tacky but news gets around fast in this small town you know, especially here at Harmony Grove. The word was out that you girls weren't speaking for several days. Debbie Sims, you know the resident cook? She said that Mr. Don Wong from the corner laundry mat told her, and Mr. Martinez's Nurse, Nurse Ida told him after he came out of his diabetic coma." Everybody knows, but Lawd I'm so glad you girls are speaking again, and I know every body here is just pleased as punch. You all not speaking was a hard pill to swallow, we were worried sick. We knew it was a hush, hush affair between you girls and all but we still couldn't help it. It broke our hearts.

Then she dismissed the gossip with a short wave of her hand, like she was shooing away a pesky old fly and said, "don't be angry', you girls are magnificent spirits with energy to spare, just like we were once-upon-a-time. I assure you, everybody here at the nursing home wish they could be your age again where there's never a dull moment of wonderful life experiences.

I declare it's so boring around here sometimes, gossip may not be nice but it brings us a little bit of excitement, especially on gloomy, depressing days like this one, people dying and all . . . and so forth and so on . . . she paused and continued, "we need excitement and you girls bring us smiles, joy and sunshine too." The old lady reminisced and smiled a crooked smile then she cheerfully changed the subject . . .

"Now tell me, have you picked out your bridesmaids dresses for your Aunt Fannie's wedding yet?"

"Yes ma'am," They said with boarder smiles than before.

"I know you're gonn'a look darling just as you always do." She said looking curiously at their shinning lips.

"We'll be attending the wedding, we are all invited to see Fannie and Neva finally jump the broom, you know. She said with great excitement, and then added,

"You girls came just in time; sist'a Williams and sist'a Smith have been asking about you girls all week long, they're sitting in the music room right now."

The girls graciously said thank you then gingerly walked down the quiet hall counting the impeccably buffed black and white checkered tiles. Silky was making large steps making sure not to step on the seams. They entered the music room where Mrs. Elsie Smith sat in her wheel chair with a brightly colored croqueted afghan draped over her legs as usual.

"Here are the little darlings" streaked Mrs. Elsie Smith, upon seeing the girls.

"I prayed that you girls would come today," she confessed.

"Well glory B, come over here girls and give me some sugar," said Miss. Willie Mae Williams smiling with her large inviting arms opened wide while her black paten leather hair shimmered. She gave each of the girls a warm smothering hug. And each girl felt the wetness from her Jheri Curl.

"My, my . . . lawd you girls sure look pretty with your matching denim overalls and matching lips too, she said with a chuckle. Pretty as a picture," said Miss. Williams.

"And you're getting so big, before you know it, you'll be all grown up."

"Yes sir're, all grown up." She said smiling.

"How's your Aunt Fannie." She asked.

"She's doing good, ma'am." said Tiffany.

"That's good, that's real good," she repeated.

"I know she's getting ready for her wedding."

"Yes, ma'am, said Brianna not really making eye contact with Miss. Williams, but obviously looking around the music room for Mr. Duffy.

Mrs. Elsie had her photo album out again showing photos of herself when she was a young girl. She carries them with her almost all the time. One was a tattered brown picture, with an old clipping from a local newspaper praising her for winning first prize in a singing audition at the Apollo theatre. She looked so pretty when she was a famous singer in her younger days. She often talked about singing in big bands wearing fabulous clothes and big jewelry at the Cotton Club in Harlem. She says that's when Harlem was at its best.

Now Mrs. Elsie and Tiffany occasionally sing gospels together as a duet for the residents at the nursing home.

Silky had a weird greasy smile pasted on her lips as she scanned the room looking for Mr. Duffy. He usually worms his way in by now with his wheel chair she thought. But there was no Mr. Duffy, not yet anyway.

"Come on Tiffany, let's sing "Sweet, Sweet Spirit". Let's get all the old geezers out of their rooms with our beautiful voices," said Mrs. Elsie wheeling her way over to the stage.

"Okay," said Tiffany, she grabbed the ear marked hymnal and turned to page 27, she knew the page number by heart. Then she helped Mrs. Elsie over to the stage.

Miss Willie Mae Williams sat at the piano while Silky and Brianna sat on each side sharing the bench with her.

As she sung, Mrs. Elsie's voice was soft and often off key. You can tell she had a great voice at one time, though. Tiffany loved singing with her. It made her feel like an honest to goodness diva. She seemed to glow, just like an angel. The fire in her young endearing voice was lovelier and stronger than ever before. Studying at the music academy was certainly making a difference.

The sun broke through the clouds, shining into the music room windows for the first time in a long time.

Upon hearing the magnificent voices of two divas, the staff at Harmony Grove made their way into the music room. Debbie Sims, the cook came in from the kitchen with a dish towel over her shoulder, Mrs. Johnson the receptionist came in with a pen and pad in her hand, the janitor came in with a mop, the delivery man from Elmira's exotic flower shop came in but without the flowers.

One by one the residents and guest gradually made their way and filled the music room to capacity. They were quietly mesmerized by Tiffany's and Mrs. Elsie's mystifying voices. Most of the guests that came in were curved over and frail, crooked from being well used in life. They walked slowly, shuffled, or wobbled in on their own. The two gentlemen who shared the bus with the girls sat in the audience with the seeing eye dog lying at their feet. A few people wore oxygen tubes in their noses, while others used the aid of a walker, crutches or canes.

Mr. Martinez was rolled in on a gurney by Nurse Ida. It was touch and go for him in the last week or so but now he's doing much better, much, much better. Caring hands wheeled in love ones and some simply wheeled themselves in, but come they did to hear the lovely voices harmoniously singing about the Sweet Spirit. Everyone except old Mr. Duffy, that is.

Smelling like blueberry gum, Brianna impatiently whispered to Miss. Willie Mae Williams, "Where's old man Duffy?"

"Where's who," the big woman asked with a frown, she bent her head down close to Brianna's face so she could hear better, while banging on the piano too.

"Um," Brianna cleared her voice and said, "Mr. Duffy, I mean, I don't see him." She said louder, after correcting herself.

"Oh dear heart," she said with a bright smile, "didn't anyone tell you girls . . . Mr. Duffy passed away last night in his sleep . . . sure did."

Her smile went away as she sadly shook her head from side to side and said in a loud whisper, "I understand he had a bad ticker you know. Poor thing, he'll miss this beautiful concert if his spirit isn't here yet."

While trying to fully digest the horrifying event, the music began to pulsate; it reminded Brianna of revival meetings at Greater Light Baptist Church. She became somewhat frightened, her little heart started pounding fast in her chest, and beads of sweat surrounded her fine wavy hair line. "Spirit, spirit . . . what's she's talking about spirit? Does this mean I gotta look for a spirit? I wonder if I will be able to see his Spirit", she thought. She wiped away the fat tears that stung her pretty brown eyes to see if Mr. Duffy's spirit was lurking in between the guest. She quickly rubbed her eyes again and again determined not to miss a thing. Silky over heard the strange conversation and became very nervous but she was convinced she'd recognize even his spirit. "He would most certainly be in his wheel chair with his thick glasses on with an irritating grin, like always." She thought. Miss Willie Mae still wasn't finished telling her ghoulish story, though.

In a loud whispered she said, "They say he had an amazing smile on his face with a fist full of chocolate chips right over his heart. That was his favorite sweets, you know. lawdy, girls, that man just loved himself some chocolate chips, she chuckled. The coroner said, he went to Glory with a fist full of love, just as peaceful as can be. That's the way I want to go when the good lawd calls me to the Sweet By and BY, you know, peaceful like . . . yeah, I want to finish strong, just like sweet Mr. Duffy." She said with joy in her heart. "lawd knows, it couldn't happen to a nicer person, yes's're. A nicer person." She said with conviction. Her face turned to sadness.

But as for the girls, the account of Mr. Duffy's death became spookier and spookier by the minutes. On the other hand, the music was sounding exceptionally celebratory this day. There was no doubt that Willie Mae Williams was feeling the pulsating beat in her veins. She banged harder and harder on the piano even harder than she rocked. By the time she finished the details of his death, she was fully engulfed in the moment, almost in a trance like state. Her smile was wider and brighter than ever before, she began to mumble the lyrics to the hymn, along with Tiffany and Mrs. Elsie.

"♫*There's a sweet, sweet spirit in this place* . . . ♫",

The discussion of Mr. Duffy's death spooked Brianna, the hair on her arms stood at attention. Willie Mae Williams acted as if Mr. Duffy's death was perfectly normal, she was comfortable talking about the dead.

Her emotions mysteriously turned to sadness again, she moaned,

"Lawd, Lawd, Lawd, what is this place gonn'a be like without sweet Mr. Duffy?

Then with a sense of urgency she confessed,

"You know girls; truck loads of pretty red carnations have been coming in all day in his honor. Yes in deed, in Mr. Duffy's honor."

At that moment a strange deep voice came out of her mouth as she fearlessly announced, "It's the Holy Ghost girls, the Holy Ghost is here, it's nothing to be afraid of now." She said, sweating profusely and without warning her large head jerked back with such uncontrolled force that her face pointed awkwardly up toward the ceiling. Both girls felt a gust of air pushed *swoosh* in their faces along with fine droplets of moisture. They didn't know if it was sweat from her body or the wetness from her Jheri Curl. The girls were frightened. They were too afraid to even look at the big women sitting next to them. By this time Willie Mae Williams began to rock almost violently, she rocked and swayed, rocked and rolled to the melodic beat. It was painful to watch, she was so unlike herself.

By this time the girls were terrified. The banging and singing wasn't melodic anymore, it was simply the shrill of madness. Brianna attempted to peek through the web of Willie Mae's large moving arms, big boobs, big belly, and massive hands that blazed across the black and white keys but it was impossible. She couldn't see Silky at the other end of the bench.

Brianna was scared out of her wits, she choked back tears and sniffled, she struggled to make eye contact with Silky.

"You, (sniffle) you, you okay, Silky? (sniffle) Silky, are you okay?" She cried in a timidly, shaken voice.

However, between the loud noise and chewing hard and fast on tasteless gum Silky didn't hear Brianna's weak cries.

She was blinded by a fury of tears of her own; everyone in the audience seemed to have blended together as one. Time and time again she struggled to hold back hot frightful tears; but it was evident she too was caught up in the moment. It was a crazy moment of desperation trying to hold on to peace that wasn't there. Everything that made sense before was absent. Silky slowly lost her grip. She wanted to run and scream, but ended up secretly praying for the strength to remain calm and normal.

Hearing the thunderous noise made the room swirled around at dizzying speed. Silky's greasy lips began to quiver; sweat and a strange restless sensation came over her body. In a last ditch effort Silky tried to regain a sense of normalcy by singing along but something unexplainable took over. In her troubled mind the song repeated one verse over and over again. She wondered if anyone else heard it. She heard it with distinctive clarity, it made no sense to her . . .

"♫*There's a sweet, sweet spirit in this place and I know it's the spirit of . . . . ?♫*",

"♫*There's a sweet, sweet spirit in this place and I know it's the spirit of . . . . ?♫*",

"♫*There's a sweet, sweet spirit in this place and I know it's the spirit of . . . . ?♫*",

The verse never revealed whose spirit it was. It sounded like an old school record that had been scratched and only played the same cluster of tuneless lyrics. In her delirium, Silky tried to complete the broken verse by shrieking out "not Mr. Duffy's spirit, not Mr. Duffy's spirit, he's not sweet." And at that moment she mysteriously fell onto the music room floor with a un-lady like thump. Pages of music scores were scattered all about. Silence replaced the celebration with a strange hush among the startled, eye bulging guest and everyone's eyes were on Silky.

The sun faded from the music room windows as gloomy, dark clouds reappeared. Silky laid there with her eyes closed in stillness. She was dazed and emotionally drained but mostly rocked to the core. Silky wasn't sure if she had fallen because of Willie Mae's wide sways and hard rocks or was she pushed by Mr. Duffy's spirit?

Chapter Eleven

Metamorphoses

Diary,

I was taking a soothing bubble bath when I overheard Momma talking on the phone to Aunt Mable. She was saying something about a tattoo and Queen Fannie's leg. She must have gotten it when we saw her on Montgomery Street passing by Young's nasty book store on her bike. That's over where Mr. Snookey's Tattoo Parlor is.

All I know is Momma was laughing, and then she said, "Girl, you got to be kidding? Is that where she put it? Well even though she's my sister, she always thought of herself as a Nubian Queen. That Fannie is something else." Momma laughed so loud, Diary, she nearly broke my eardrums, and I was all the way in the bathroom. When she hung up the phone, Momma walked by the bathroom and peeked in. I asked her what was she laughing about, she said, "Never you mind, little girl." Then, she started laughing again, saying, "Lawd have mercy!"

I didn't really care anyway, I was thinking about what happened at Harmony Grove the other day, with Mr. Duffy dying and all, and the strange feeling that came over me, so I wrote this poem of how it made me feel.

Dang, that freaked me out
That was a spooky time
Miss Willie Mae Williams hooped and hollered
I witnessed her tortured cries
The piano lady rocked and rolled
She exploded out of control
But I truly believe I met Mr. Duffy
I met him soul to soul.

The sun boldly came out, blazing, spreading streams of hot rays across the sky and trees and then seemingly settling firmly on Fannie's property. And if that wasn't enough, a rainbow arched from the heavens and ended at the corner of Fannie's evenly planted collard greens. "This is a blessed day," thought Fannie, "a mighty blessed day." Laying in bed, her mind darted in different directions from one situation to another. She was pressed for time.

It would take only a matter of hours for the grass to dry and the muddy areas would firm up a bit. The garden and orchards were in full bloom. Even the birds decided to come out and chirp a few tunes.

After hearing the loud doorbell, Fannie stumbled out of bed in her bare feet; she peeked out from her bedroom blinds.

It was real early in the morning, and there stood Mrs. Crump carrying a suitcase, a suite bag and a few plastic grocery bags full of stuff. She had arrived early to help Fannie make this day a perfect day for the bride.

Hmmm, it's unusual for the sun to shine so bright this early in the morning, thought Fannie. Then, she smiled. This was the best sign, indicating that her prayers were being answered. "Thank you, Lawd. Thank you. Thank you, Lawd!" she said relieved.

"Oh, good," Fannie said upon seeing Mrs. Crump standing down at the front door. "I'll be down in a second."

Fannie slid her freshly manicured feet into the furry slippers. She didn't see Earl, which warned her that he was probably under the bed waiting for her to move her feet, for the thrill of attacking the swinging tails. Pearl, was sitting beside her on the bed purring and grooming her paws. Fannie took a long look at the slippers on her feet, and decided, "Not today, I'm gonna put on my new bedroom slippers."

She walked to the bedroom closet in her bare feet and took out a white shoebox that had a pair of brand new slippers inside. Fannie took the leopard printed mules with the three-inch heel out of the box and slipped them on. They're sharp. She said to herself, real sharp, indeed.

Almost instantly Fannie radiated a certain flair for the finer things that life had to offer, she stood taller and walked taller with a certain sway.

"They feel real good, just like they're already broken in," she said with a smile. When she moved her feet this time, Earl jumped out from under the bed, but retreated as fast as he started when he realized he didn't have a tail to attack. Fannie looked at the furry nuisance and grinned. She playfully stuck her tongue out at him. And said, "So there."

She had a different agenda for this day and it didn't involve a cat chasing behind her. "Today is my day, Earl. You hear?" She said, pointing that index finger as her hips swayed down the stairs.

Fannie saw Mrs. Crump's large silhouette through the stain glass door.

"Hi, Mrs. Crump," smiled Fannie giving her a heartwarming hug.

"Well, good morning to the bride. I hope you slept well last night, dear," Mrs. Crump said, smiling and walking into the foyer.

"I desperately prayed for sleep last night. I had a rather restless night."

"Oh, honey. I know all too well," said Mrs. Crump. "I know firsthand how you feel. I felt the same way the day of my wedding, it was many years ago, but I remembered it like it was yesterday." She laid her packages down and took off her dry raincoat. A pretty red silk scarf covered her large hair rollers.

Fannie took her coat, saying, "here let me help you with that."

She noticed that Mrs. Crump had a pair of khaki pants on. For as long as she has known Mrs. Crump, this was the first time she'd ever seen her in pants.

It was obvious she wasn't fashion conscious for herself, thought Fannie.

Fannie noticed her pants were hiked up too far over her waist, causing the hem to hang way above her ankles.

Ashamed of her thoughts, Fannie decided to remain nonjudgmental. It was the proper thing to do. If everyone was the same, the world would be flat out boring. It takes variety to make life interesting. Fannie stood thinking. Yes, variety is the spice of life. She concluded to herself.

"You need any help with anything?" Fannie asked, taking the suitcase out of her hand.

"No dear, I think we got everything."

"You got the tea on, Fannie? You know I've got to unwind a bit before we get busy around here."

"Good as done," Fannie said and quickly went to put the glass kettle on, while Mrs. Crump got comfortable.

"Fannie," said Mrs. Crump, "those are some fancy slippers you have on your feet."

"Oh, thank you. Aren't they simply fabulous? They're a far cry from those other ones," she said, pointing one foot to the front. "They make me feel special on this special day."

"I know what you mean." Mrs. Crump said. "You should see the shoes I'm going to wear at the wedding and reception. I brought them two days ago. They cost me a pretty penny, too. I'm going to strut my stuff today, I'm going to have a good time. You only live once, you know?" She said half giggling and half smiling.

"Mrs. Crump, would you like some collard greens with your brewed green tea?" Fannie offered.

By eight a.m., the house was teaming with folks running in and out of the house. Even though Fannie had plenty of room in her back yard, there were hips bumping into other folks' hips and elbows swinging from here to there. Around the property was a gridlock of parked cars of every color, shape and size. Of course, Mrs. Crump was the first to come, so she was parked conveniently on the cobblestone driveway near to Fannie's bike and bike stand. Everyone else had to double park or parked down a ways.

Elmira was also among the first to arrive. She conveniently parked her large van behind Mrs. Crump's utility vehicle. Elmira's four employees, who rode with her, began decorating immediately when they reached the backyard. All you heard from them is whispering voices conferring with each other, as they darted around the same area like worker bees, focused on their job of making Fannie's backyard into a dreamy wonderland.

They interlaced the outside of the gazebo with streams of blue and white silk ribbons and bows. Even the prickly bushes were adored in festive white ribbon, the same kind of ribbon that was wrapped around the beams of the gazebo in candy cane fashion. The freshly painted white porch had blue ribbon draped like Christmas garland, from one post to the neighboring post accentuated with a vibrant color of primroses in the middle. A large yellow and white striped tent was pitched up on one side of the yard. Under the tent, caterers scurried to arrange long serving tables that would accommodate the smorgasbord of tasty edibles. The main table had an elaborate iridescent blue-skirted tablecloth with cream-colored roses pinned along the bottom of the skirt. An arrangement of cream-colored roses and baby's breath centered each table. The skirted round table on the left was being specially prepared for the five tiered wedding cake made by Sweeney the pastry chef.

The other round table on the right side sat one large shiny coffee urn perked ready for fresh brewed coffee; the smaller urn was hot water perked for spice tea or hot chocolate. Behind the tables were several ice chests lined up and filled to the brim with ice and soft drinks.

Someone had already fired up the bar-be-que pit, preparing it for an assortment of meats.

The R & B band from Kathy's Bar and Grill was the last to arrive. They played soothing music for the last of the workers who cheerfully swayed to the rhythm while putting the finishing touches on the lavishly decorated gazebo. It certainly was the center piece of the wedding and the grand reception to follow.

Not yet dressed, Fannie ventured out to greet the workers. She knew many of them very well. With her hair wrapped underneath an oversized white terry towel, she browsed around smiling and thanked each well-wisher. She couldn't help but marvel at her yard. It had been transformed into something wonderfully different. "A metamorphosis", thought Fannie. Then she noticed two small holes in the fence where Neva hastily mended it back after Fruity had his free meal of collard greens. One hole was near the top the other was at the bottom.

Elmira broke Fannie's concentration when she said, "Hi girl, it's only a matter of hours before you officially become Mrs. Fannie Schine." She said smiling with a prominent nose and gold tooth.

You can tell her Jheri Curl was freshly done; it appeared to be wet.

Smiling, Fannie went over and nervously hugged her outspoken friend.

In their embrace, Elmira whispered, "You're going to be just fine, my dear friend. How are the girls doing, Fannie? Are they speaking yet? I heard Brianna boo-hoo'd herself to sleep the other night worried about not looking like her cousins."

"Mercy, Elmira, you know those girls mean the world to me. I didn't want to cause any problems for them. Well, I'm getting a little jittery, but I know everything will be just fine. Look . . . see," she pointed, "the sun is coming out to shine in a big way on my special day. And I'm marrying my longtime friend, Neva Schine." Then, she said, "I hope the girls forgive me for causing them pain."

"Ahhh, come on, Fannie, you're the one who makes their fantasies come true; you know that. This will be a remarkable experience for them."

"We'll see, my dear friend, we'll see." Fannie said wishfully.

"Let me go now. They'll be here any minute now, all dressed and ready to walk down this mahvahlous aisle."

"Okay, okay." Elmira said in a loud whisper, smiling with one last hug before Fannie disappeared up the steps and into the back door, making her way up to the magic room.

Chapter Twelve

Smile for the Camera

Diary,

I don't have time to write anything today on account of the wedding and all. Oh yeah . . . I asked my Momma would she weave a few strands of ash blonde hair in each of my braids for the wedding. She said okay, so she weaved them in for me and it looks so good against my brown complexion and my real hair is a lot longer too almost as long as the blonde extensions. I look simply mahvahlous . . . ha, ha, ha. Everybody who saw my new "do" said it suits me just fine . . . Queen Fannie especially approved! Guess who came to town for the wedding? Justin Brooks and his family, I think Tiffany has a crush on him.

My daddy said I can use his camera to take my own pictures at the wedding, so Diary, this is going to be too cool, 'll I have my very own personal scrapbook full of wedding pictures, plus I'll have you, with all the details.

Diary I think we make a good pair, I do all the writing and you provide all the dreamy blue pages.

Volunteers from church remained under the tent, feverishly working on last minute touches.

Satisfied with their new look, the bridesmaids nervously huddled together and cried happy tears as Mable chauffeured them to Herbert Way.

Peering through the rearview mirror, Mable smiled and said, "You girls look so pretty, just like royalty." With all the excitement it was hard to believe the girls were at a loss for words.

The trio blushed, and then grinned, Silky spoke first and said, "Thank you, Aunt Mable."

Hump, Fannie was right to suggest each girl pick her own dress style, thought Mable. They reminded her of majestic bluebirds.

Upon arrival, the girls made their way through the fancy doors and into the gloomy overly knickknack spare room on the parlor floor.

Elmira emerged from the back yard carrying a green plastic bag, the front had her store's logo was written in white. It read *IT'S BETTER WITH FLOWERS. Elmira's Exotic Flower Shop* with the address.

"Where are all the little ladies?" Elmira called slightly out of breath.

"Here we are Elmira, in the spare bed room." Ruth said.

Elmira dramatically stopped in her tracks when she saw the girls all dressed up.

She said, "Excuse me for staring, but I haven't seen so much glamour in one room in all my days. You girls look beautiful." She said grinning.

"Really?" ask, Tiffany, in a high pitch voice.

"Really," Confirmed Elmira with one hand on the side of her face.

"Thank you, Miss Elmira," chimed all three girls, still holding back their excitement for the anticipated celebration.

Elmira rummaged through her green plastic bag and handed the girls little bouquets adorned with blue carnations, baby's breath and yellow primroses. Wrapped around was some other greenery with the accentuation of a sizable blue bow with long streams of silk ribbon that will cascade midway down their gowns.

"Ohhhh," was all the cousins could say when they held their bouquets.

"Where's Aunt Fannie?" asked Tiffany excited.

"Your Aunt Fannie is up in the magic room getting dressed. Mrs. Crump is there to help her," said Freda while fussing over a group of beads on Silky's braids.

"Tiffany, please find an outlet and plug in the curling iron. This curl here needs to be curled a little tighter; it's starting to droop," said Ruth fingering Tiffany's shoulder length hair.

"Maybe it's too humid for them to stay curled," Ruth complained.

Worried, Tiffany looked in the mirror and said, "Oh no, Mom, maybe it is too humid outside, this might be one of my bad hair days." She said with some agitation.

"We'll just do the best we can with what we have. Hand me the curling iron baby, it should be nice and hot by now." Ruth worked feverishly to put the curls back into Tiffany's hair.

Elmira said, "Don't let me forget now," she carried a medium sized white cardboard box she managed to pry the top off, inside were three delicately decorated crowns protected by white tissue paper. The crowns were made of carnations in the same contrasting blues with little yellow primroses and baby breath scattered all around.

"Here girls, here are your head pieces for your pretty locks. Your Aunt Fannie designed them and your bouquet; she even designed her own bouquet. Let's see if they need adjusting." She said, wiping sweat from her face with a laced trimmed hanky.

"Wow," said the girls again in complete excitement. Each mother arranged their daughter's hair to accommodate the perfectly fitted crowns.

"Is Aunt Fannie wearing a crown too? Maybe we'll be able to see her real hair for the first time." Brianna asked in a most sincere way.

"Yeah," smiled Tiffany.

"I can't say, she designed her own new head piece, you know, so it will be a surprise to everyone, even me." said Elmira.

"And here are blue corsages for the mothers." Elmira said without missing a beat. She handed them out. They were the same pretty colors as the girls' bouquets. Freda and Mable wore theirs on the wrist, while Tiffany pinned it on her mother's left shoulder.

Elmira mentioned that the next time she gets the chance to talk with them, Fannie and Neva would be husband and wife. As she rushed out back, Elmira was beyond herself with excitement. She took off her green smock, showing a lime colored crepe de shin party dress, and said, "Then the celebration will be in full swing!"

Brianna nervously peeped out the bedroom window. The backyard looked like a wonderland with all the exotic flowers and trimmings and a well-dressed gazebo too.

There were sounds of light laughter as friends and family members arrived. They greeted each other by hugging one another and shaking hands as they took their seats.

Reverend Katrill stood in the gazebo with his black robe on holding his big black Bible with one hand and wiping his brow with a large white handkerchief in the other.

Silky stopped and took a long look before she said in a low voice, "There's Ms. Willie Mae Williams sitting in the third row with Miss Elise Smith." The other two girls glanced at each other, not saying anything.

Silky never mentioned anything about what happened at the nursing home or Mr. Duffy's death. She wanted to forget that day; it still made her feel uneasy and ashamed.

"Oh yeah, and there's Mr. Spiegel from the supermarket."

"Yeah," the girls giggled.

"There's my daddy sitting in the front row." Said Silky

"Who's that sitting next to him Silky? He looks like somebody I know." Brianna said, squinting her eyes to see what she could see better. Both Tiffany and Silky looked at the seated guest, and spotted the familiar looking fellow.

"Oh snap, it's Cool Aid, with a hair cut!" Said Tiffany and Silky together with wide eyes. They held their hands over their mouths as if they were going to bust the seams of their pretty dresses if they laughed too hard.

Freda, Mable, and Ruth heard the commotion and tripped over each other running to take a peek from the adjacent window.

The ugly, dark pea green curtains opened with a pull cord letting in streaks of sunlight, Mable lifted up one blind and peeped out; she spotted him instantly,

"My, my, he is a nice looking young man." She whispered still gazing out.

"He sure is, girl," Ruth agreed.

Freda looked and commented, "Well, well, well, he cut off those boyish braids. She paused and said, "he does look real handsome, Silky."

"I told you he was terrific," said Silky with a smile of confidence.

Freda corrected her and said, "I said he looked handsome, I didn't say anything about him being terrific!"

All the guests were seated. Some of the women were fanning while Neva looked dapper for this special occasion. He wore a black tuxedo and a cowboy hat that was adorned with a band of gold. His tuxedo jacket concealed the gold suspenders. His pants were long enough to partially show his cowboy boots that Fannie bought him as a wedding present.

Neva joined the Reverend in the gazebo, while the photographer stood on the side patiently waiting for the bridal party to walk down the make shift aisle.

Mrs. Crump rushed into the spare room to admire the girls for the first time that day.

"Hoooo" said the trio, putting their hands up to their mouths again. They looked at Mrs. Crump, in her peach silk blend dress, with matching satin high-heeled sandals with red nail polish on each toe. The wide-brimmed peach colored hat covered the top of her silver and black hair that curled to her shoulders. It was an incredible transformation. She even had hazel green contact lenses on. They didn't think Mrs. Crump could ever look so nice. In fact they wondered if that was the real Mrs. Crump.

"My word, you look wonderful," said Freda and Mable together.

"Thank you, ladies, and you too look wonderful, simply glamorous." She said blushing.

"Okay, girls," said Mable still staring at Mrs. Crump, with a curious smile. "It's time for us to take our seats outside. When you hear the musical cord girls, that will be your cue to walk out. Okay?"

Heavy footsteps could be heard running into the house. They reached the door to the room. It was Silky's father, Leon. With a sparkle in his eyes, the medium sized man said, "the veteran ladies in this here room sure look good," he said with a grin. But his face lit up when he said, "but the younger ladies here look like run way models, especially my little Silky Blue," he said, with a wide grin.

Silky was tickled all over with joy, and was happy to see that sparkle in his eyes again.

"Okay, Leon, you got to go. It's almost time for them to march," Freda said. Leon kissed Freda lightly on the lips and said "okay darling I'm out'a here." He rushed out closing the door behind him and made a burp at the same time. Silky and Tiffany flashed an eye in each others direction and giggled.

Freda shook her head in disapproval but paid him little attention as she stared at Mrs. Crump. Was it really the same woman they met at Fannie's house for the girls fitting? If so, she looks ten years younger, she thought.

"Mommy, you look so beautiful." Tiffany said, in a tone of nervous exhaustion.

"Thank you, my dear. I feel like this is going to be a wonderful day for Fannie, a wonderful day for everybody." She said.

As the sisters and sister-in-law rushed out to their seats, the cousins could hear them in agreement saying, "Lawd, I don't know how Fannie pulled this one off, but she did a magnificent job."

Now that the coast was clear, Pearl and Earl emerged from under the bed and sat on top of the purple and green comforter where all the elaborately wrapped gifts were. They seem to have wanted the girl's attention.

"I guess they're waiting for us to perform," laughed Silky.

Brianna looked around then took out her blueberry lip-gloss from her bag and each of the bridesmaids took turns spreading the glossy stuff on their little lips. "Let's forget about the dark brown lip liner," said Brianna

"Okay," replied Tiffany.

"But it's the finishing touch my lips need." Silky said.

Silky carefully outlined her lips very lightly with dark brown lip liner and pursed her lips tightly together to give it that smudge look.

Suddenly they heard their cue from the piano.

"That's our cue," Tiffany said giggling nervously.

Then they all giggled through a fast group hug before they walked out into the sunlight and into the quiet breeze. The smell of delicious food and the fragrance of exotic flowers mingled together complimenting each other in a most festive way.

The bridal music played as the girls walked slowly down the aisle among a chorus of "woooo's and ahhhhs." Brianna was the first, Tiffany was second and Silky was the third to walk to the front. The photographer stooped down a little to get a full shot of Brianna.

Her straight spaghetti strapped gown gave her that mature look she was looking for. It was the right length for the peek-a-boo slit on the side, while still hiding her stockings. The darts in the front accentuated her waistline very nicely, showing off her slight curves. Brianna looked like an angel. Her dark wavy hair was relaxed. It was longer than ever before reaching all the way down to the middle of her back. It even shimmered in the bright sunlight. She smiled as she stepped in tune, until she saw her father and brother sitting next to her mother in the second row. Brianna was beside herself with joy. She stepped out of rhythm to the music but quickly regained her composure. She blew a kiss to her father. He pretended to catch it and planted on his cheek.

Not far from Brianna, Tiffany smiled, looking every bit like her grandmother, Dear. She was careful and took baby steps just like Mrs. Crump said. The crown of flowers was perfect for her long flowing brown hair that amazingly held its curls. She indeed felt like a star as her short see through cape blew slightly in the wind.

Mrs. Crump was good at making sure the hem was ankle length just the length she wanted. Tiffany was smiling wide enough to see a mouth full of metal braces. She knew a lot of the guest who where there, and a few she couldn't remember. Much to her surprise, she saw an eye peeking through the hole in the fence and at a bottom hole was the snout of a dog. "Cecil Cartwright and Fruity," she said laughing to herself.

Behind Tiffany, Silky appeared clumsy at first but regained her composure and gave Mrs. Crump the oomph she had suggested at rehearsal. By adding a little bounce in her step Silky was right on time. Her fabulous baby blue knee high dress gathered nicely at the waist with the matching sash which gave Silky the look she wanted. It made her brown, shapely legs appear even longer. She wore blue beads on her braids as they matched the blue in her head piece perfectly.

As she neared the front smiling from ear to ear with shiny lips, she paused a second or two giving the photographer the opportunity to take her picture while showing off her legs. In her heart she *was* a run way model, with plenty of finesse to spare.

As a male usher rolled out the white runner for the bride's entrance, friends and family stood up holding their breath as the piano player played Wagner's "Bridal Chorus."

The sun shined brightly as Neva stood in the gazebo with nervous anticipation of finally marrying his best friend. And even though he had a serious look on his sweaty face, his heart rejoiced with a spirit he'd never felt before. No one was more ready or happier than he was.

The melody of the piano broke the silence. Fannie's guests stood mesmerized acknowledging her charm and beauty. Goosebumps covered the bridal party's arms, as they looked on in complete awe at their aunt.

The bride floated into view for all to see elegantly dressed in a dreamy white satin gown. It was neither gaudy nor plain but acceptable as far as Freda was concerned. Fannie's neck was covered with lace the antique wedding gown was layered in three layers. Each layer was heavily beaded with jewels and pearls, rhinestones and crystals ending with a small baby blue scalloped hem that was taken from the same fabric of the girls' dresses. The dress was just short enough to see Fannie's new white cowboy boots peeking from under as she floated towards her handsome groom.

Fannie borrowed the locket form Freda the one with the pictures of their parents inside; it was most befitting for the occasion.

Her new headpiece was a fancy African wrap made from an iridescent white fabric. It covered her entire head! One end of the wrap swayed in the air while the other end laid softly on her beaded shoulder.

With the hands on the clock going upward for good luck, Fannie indeed walked down the aisle keeping up with the tradition of something old, something new, something borrowed and something blue.

The birds and squirrels on Herbert Way were quietly peering through the thick branches and green leaves of the pecan tree. They seemed to sense this amazing moment belonged to Fannie as she gracefully walked down the aisle smiling.

Fannie smelled the earth and felt the soft breeze blowing across her face. She knew that all was well. She had that perfect look, the same look the girls saw when they hid behind the huckleberry bush that day. Their Aunt Fannie was happy.

Fannie looked toward the end of the white runner and there was Neva Schine beaming with joy. "Look at what the Lawd has done," Fannie murmured behind her happy made-up face. "He certainly out did himself this time, with this beautiful day and there at the end of this white runner is where my sunshine begins."

Tiffany, Silky and Brianna couldn't be happier. They were their new independent selves now, and still cousins and best friends too. Watching their Aunt Fannie making a statement of her own, by marrying Uncle Schine, they knew he was the right choice because Aunt Fannie was always right!

In the end, they all smiled for the camera.

Epilogue

Diary,

This is an appropriate time for a poem.

Parades of stars graced the sky
For the fanciest Queen of all
She proudly recited her wedding vows
Without a hitch or flaw
Ordinary is not her style
But unique in every way
She had her emerald collards
Arranged in her floral spray
And even served the fresh bouquets
On the buffet line
I knew she married her best friend
His name is Neva Schine

Diary we had a good time dancing and eating.. The castle never looked so nice; it was all lit up like a grand Christmas tree. There were bright lights shining all around and all the guests were smiling and some laughed real loud. Everything glowed with happiness.

Cool Aid and my daddy talked about basketball mostly all night, they were on their second plate of bar-be-que ribs and collard greens.

I danced with Justin, we both were happy to dance with each other. "Wow"!

When Tiffany wasn't dancing on the limbo line, she was looking for Aunt Ruth. My daddy finally jumped on line, he's the eighth one. See? He's the one with the shiny forehead behind Ms. Elmira.

This picture here is Mr. Snookey showing off all his tattoos to Ms. Hazel Nut, while she's doing the funky chicken.

I have a picture with Aunt Ruth catching the wedding bouquet.

And guess what . . . . It was made with tender young collard greens, white lilies and blue carnations. Wrapped around the stems were blue and white silk ribbon tied in a bow. It did look good though, even if it was a bouquet of her best collard greens! Nobody was surprised, it's just Aunt Fannie's style.

Later on that day, I took a picture of Aunt Ruth and Mr. Eli swinging on the porch swing. They were talking but mostly smiling and looking into each other's eyes. Look, you can see Aunt Ruth is holding tight to the bridal bouquet she caught. (I mean Collard Greens, ha, ha, ha,).

I got a picture of Brianna dancing with her father. Here she is . . . she's wearing the pretty turquoise bracelet her father gave her. See, I told you she wears it only on special occasions.

Here's another picture of Brianna holding on to her father's hand for dear life, while Uncle Ned's other hand held on to Aunt Mable's. Uncle Ned looked the same, only he has a graying ponytail and his stomach is bigger. Stuck-on-himself Jabari, has the reputation for being a hunk in college and a party animal too. His mustache is much thicker now, but he's still a cute peanut head to me.

I took a picture showing Mrs. Crump and Mr. Sweeney on the limbo line. It was amazing, Diary. She just giggled all through the reception. Even while helping my Momma and my aunts clean up after the reception. She was still giggling and laughing 'til tears filled her eyes! I wonder if she had the same brand of sparkling cider as we had.

Here's a picture of Momma fanning her face. She's finally sitting down after being on her feet all day. As you can see, she has her shoes off. Momma and Reverend Katrill both have a big, big bowl of collard greens with sparkling cider on the side.

I was teary eyed when Uncle Schine started loading Queen Fannie's leopard printed luggage set into his antique silver Rolls Royce. After they jumped over the broom, we threw brown rice because that's what our Queen wanted. Then, they left town for their honeymoon. I wonder if Uncle Schine saw Queen Fannie's tattoo yet. I know I didn't! But I just knew that things would never be the same again at the castle.

Diary, I have to confess, I'm embarrassed about what I said about Mr. Duffy and how I wanted to jack him up and all. But I can't help think if I was right about his touches or was I making something out of nothing. Anyway, I was also confused about the two older men who were on the bus that afternoon. Not to mention that they were even in the audience at Harmony Grove made it a strange situation.

I asked Mrs. Johnson, Harmony Groves secretary, did she know who they were, 'cause she know everybody and keeps up with the gossip. She told me that they were Mr. Duffy's first cousins. They had been raised together. She even said that they were best friends, too.

"No way," I said. I was mortified. She nodded her head and said with a smile, "Just like you and your cousins." Then, she added, "When they got older they weren't able to see each other as much as they would have liked because the three of them lived in different states because of their careers and families and now they have health challenges. Then she said something that blew my mind. She said that they talked to each other nearly every day on three way calls. And those calls really made Mr. Duffy's day, just to speak to his cousins, made him feel young and loved again.

Mrs. Johnson didn't stop there; she had more to tell. She said, "Everybody knew that you girls didn't approve of the names he called you, but they were names of endearment. Then she said, "Let me explain. One of his cousin's wife was named Olivia, and the other wife was named Ver'nilla. However, Mr. Duffy's wife's name was Sara. Well Mr. Duffy and his wife owned a candy store, and chocolate chips were their specialty. Every piece of candy was made with chocolate chips, or had a chocolate chip on the top for the perfect decoration. And since he—loved his wife so very much and she was a pretty chocolate women, why he use to even call her chocolate chip."

Dang, Diary I know I really messed up. I didn't want to hear anymore. I didn't want to believe that I was so stupid. I now know that calling me chocolate chip had nothing to do with me being a mere morsel or about my chocolate complexion. Even if it did, I know now he meant it in love. Gosh I'm confused; the truth made me feel good . . . I feel shameful though, sort'a like Fruity did, only I don't have a hole to crawl into.

I'm mostly embarrassed and angry; I can't believe we had Mr. Duffy all wrong or maybe I'm the one who had him all wrong. I haven't told my cousin's yet, mostly because I don't know what to say for the second time in my life! Maybe it will be a secret just between you and me Diary, okay?

It is the beginning of the end for me and my cousins being three peas in a pod, you know, dressing the same and all. Queen Fannie was right, it was a liberating experience. And I got some good news. My daddy finally thinks Cool aid is terrific. I always knew he was terrific.

Writing in a Diary is not as dumb as I thought it would be. It's packed with some good stuff. I can't believe I wrote all this stuff. It makes me laugh, makes me think, sometimes cry. It reminds me that the family is the best part of my life. It's fun in a weird sort of way. I do treasure you Diary; you have some of my best secrets concealed between these wonderful pages of precious memories.

Oh, just between you and me, before the wedding, I had a chance to sneak up to the magic room and dab a little bit of Queen Fannie's tea rose perfume behind my ears.

P.S. We never did see her real hair though, or at least my cousins haven't. It's still a mystery to them. I didn't tell them that I saw her real hair one day when she stooped over to tie her gym shoes. Under the blonde wig, I saw more blonde hair. Or was that gray? I really don't know for sure, but I felt a little weird seeing her real hair for the first time.

P.P.S. Guess what, with the excitement of the wedding and all, I forgot about my plastic sandwich bag with my, you know what inside, for just in case remember? Well, wouldn't you know I'd need it on the very day Queen Fannie got married . . . of all days!

But my Momma was prepared for me with designer wings. Yep, I finally got my magic moment!

See, I'm a grown woman now. Well, at least a young lady. Hallelujah!

Silky

CPSIA information can be obtained
at www.ICGtesting.com
Printed in the USA
FFHW01n1648090918
48253374-52032FF

9 781477 297933